WHEN SHADOWS FALL

WHEN SHADOWS FALL

KATE FELLOWES

THORNDIKE
CHIVERS

This Large Print edition is published by Thorndike Press, Waterville, Maine, USA and by BBC Audiobooks Ltd, Bath, England.
Thorndike Press, a part of Gale, Cengage Learning.

The text of this Large Print edition is unabridged.
Other aspects of the book may vary from the original edition.
Set in 16 pt. Plantin.
Printed on permanent paper.

LIBRARY OF CONGRESS CATALOGING-IN-PUBLICATION DATA

Fellowes, Kate.
  When shadows fall / by Kate Fellowes.
    p. cm. — (Thorndike Press large print gentle romance)
  ISBN-13: 978-1-4104-1099-3 (hardcover : alk. paper)
  ISBN-10: 1-4104-1099-4 (hardcover : alk. paper)
  1. Murder—Investigation—Fiction. 2. Large type books.
I. Title.
PS3606.E3887W47 2008
813'.6—dc22   2008033287

BRITISH LIBRARY CATALOGUING-IN-PUBLICATION DATA AVAILABLE

Published in 2008 in the U.S. by arrangement with Swimming Kangaroo Books.
Published in 2009 in the U.K. by arrangement with Swimming Kangaroo Books.

U.K. Hardcover: 978 1 408 42115 4 (Chivers Large Print)
U.K. Softcover: 978 1 408 42116 1 (Camden Large Print)

Printed in the United States of America
1 2 3 4 5 6 7 12 11 10 09 08

To Darling Neal —
My second self,
best earthly companion
and partner in crime

CHAPTER ONE

"Gretchen! Pick up the phone!" My best friend's voice came from my answering machine. "Stop screening your calls. I know you're there!"

I groaned and dislodged the washcloth from over my eyes. Slowly I let one hand emerge from beneath the water, reaching over the edge of the tub for the phone.

"Sandy." It was a statement. I said it again. "Sandy, what?"

Even when I was prepared for it, her enthusiasm was startling. And tonight, she was excited. Oh, dear.

"Gretchen, I've got fabulous news! It happened by accident. I could hardly believe it and — well, the upshot is, I've found you a job!"

I'd been listening with one ear, concentrating on the rise and fall of the bubbles as I took deep, even breaths. Now, though, I sat up straight so quickly some water sloshed onto the floor.

"No? Really? Tell me!"

The air felt cold on my wet skin, but I hardly registered the goosebumps. A job! Any job! Oh, hallelujah!

"Okay." Sandy inhaled audibly before launching into an explanation. "I was working late at the university. We're doing that famous authors lecture series, remember? Anyway, I got to chatting with Elaine from World Affairs, and she told me about this guy who used to be a professor at the school. He quit and wrote a best seller! Lived in Europe for a while, I guess. She thinks it was in Tuscany. Or Vienna. She couldn't recall."

"Anyway . . ."

"Yes, anyway, he's back in the area, working on a new book and he's looking for a secretary slash research assistant. Naturally, I thought of you. It would be perfect. I have his phone number right here. Got a pen?"

"Actually, no. I'm in the tub." I tucked the phone into my neck and stood up, reaching for a towel and dripping. "Give me a minute. Tell me more. What's his name?"

There was a pause on the line. "His name? Sure. It's John David Honeycutt." She said it fast, making it one long word.

But I wasn't fooled.

"Wait a minute. Honeycutt as in The Honeycutts?" I gave the words capital letters.

The Honeycutt family was the Midwest equivalent of the Kennedys. Rich, glamorous and peppered with scandal, the Honeycutts lived very public lives. Even if you didn't want to know about them, you did. It was difficult to avoid the headlines and the gossip.

"I don't remember any Honeycutt who was a serious scholar," I told Sandy. "A couple of lawyers, the congressman and that one who tried to be a singer. No professors."

"No, this one's sort of a second stringer. His father was brother to the really famous one — old Bill Honeycutt. That makes the professor cousin to the lawyers and the congressman and the singer." Sandy had obviously been working overtime getting the family tree straight. Now, she pushed on. "So, got that pen handy? I'll give you the number."

I knotted the tie on my robe, cinching it tighter than it needed to be. "Hmmm." I was thoughtful, wondering what it would be like to work for minor royalty. Could be good, could be bad. Definitely interesting. I moved down the hall to the kitchen and my notepad. "Okay, shoot."

She rattled off the digits quickly, then repeated them in slow, even cadence to make sure I'd gotten it right.

Clasping the paper as if it were a winning lottery ticket, I offered up thanks. "Sandy," I promised, "if this works out, I'll take you to lunch at the overpriced restaurant of your choice."

She chuckled, then scoffed. "You don't have to do that. Just pay me the money you owe. I believe it now comes to —"

"Yes, yes," I cut her off. "I know how much." There is nothing more humbling than borrowing money from your best friend. Which brought another question to mind.

"Hey, Sandy, how much does this job pay? Any idea? I suppose because the family's so rich, they'll be really cheap," I speculated, drawing dollar signs all around the phone number.

"Oh, I don't know about that, Gretchen." Ever the optimist. "But, in any event, beggars can't be choosers." When I didn't reply, she added, "No offense."

I shrugged, only mildly irritated by her succinct description of my life's situation. "None taken. It's just that the truth hurts."

"Oh, Gretch!" she gushed with sympathy.

"It's not so bad. You got a raw deal, that's all. And that job was never right for you anyway. Too stifling for someone creative. It was just a matter of time before you quit, you know that." A pause. "But they fired you first."

I shut my eyes, held them closed for a few long seconds. Ancient history. This was all ancient history now. My telemarketing career had been brief. It turns out the company really did monitor calls for quality, and I was judged to be too honest for my own good. But I just couldn't talk folks into spending money I knew they didn't have. "Maybe you should sleep on your decision," I'd tell them and that was definitely not company policy. I changed the subject.

"Maybe I'll give this guy a call right now, before it gets too late."

"Good idea." Sandy seemed to welcome the transition. "I'll let you go. Let me know how it turns out, okay?"

"Well, of course! And Sandy?"

"Yes?"

"Thanks, again."

She could tell I was sincere by the tone of my voice. I did my best to convey how grateful I was, not just for the job lead, or the emergency loan, but for everything she'd

11

always done and been for me. We'd been friends for twenty years, since the first day of kindergarten. She knew me better than I knew myself, and she knew I wasn't one for elaborate emotional displays.

Now, she fluffed off my moment of heartfelt honesty. "You'll get the job, Gretch," her assurance came in a rush. "Who knows, maybe you'll even get Honeycutt!"

"What does that mean?"

"I asked Elaine. He's single!" She was giggling when she hung up the phone.

CHAPTER TWO

Standing at the mirror, I combed the tangles from my hair, wondering where Sandy got her romantic notions. Honestly, she was hopeless, always fixing people up — or trying to — always falling too hard and getting her heart broken. But she kept bouncing back from every knight who turned into a cad and every dreamboat that gave her nightmares.

Not me. Once was enough. True love came, swept me away with the force of a rain-swollen river — then washed me up onto the rocks. It had happened a good five years ago during my last semester of college, but the memory was still raw around the edges. I flinched now as his name flashed through my mind. That name I never wanted to hear again. It was better, I thought, to think about another name.

John David Honeycutt.

He hadn't been home when I'd called a

few minutes before, so I'd left a message that had probably sounded a little too desperate. Maybe he'd decide it was merely enthusiasm making me talk too fast.

"Yes, really," I said aloud, grimacing at my reflection. "Well, get a grip at the interview — if you get one. This could be a golden opportunity!"

My image nodded back at me, and I noticed a faint blush in my cheeks. High excitement at the prospect of gainful employment. I'd have to make sure it was there if and when I met Mr. Honeycutt. The hint of color made me look eager and responsive. And that unexpected spark in my eyes brought green into the deep brown. I blinked, looking again and feeling pleased.

I'd put my hair up, twirling the shoulder-length locks around my fingers until they coiled into a semblance of a French twist. I'd add my real gold earrings. The new red blouse from the discount mall would bring out the red in my brown hair, and I'd wear the black skirt that made me look taller than five foot six.

It was easier to decide what to wear than what to say.

"Why do you want this job?" I could hear him asking that standard interview question.

Why, indeed?

How wonderful it would be to be honest. "I don't want this job! I don't want any job! I'm an artist. I want to devote my time to my art. Follow my heart! Use my talent! I want to paint!" I was shaking my fists, raising my voice, repeating out loud the thoughts I'd had a million times.

But artists starve in their garrets, next to playwrights and novelists. Truly, I was thinner than I'd been four months ago, when my last job had ended unexpectedly.

Clearing my throat, I practiced a more tempered response. "I've always had an eye for detail." Well, that was certainly true enough. "I have a great fondness for history and recognize its importance to the present." Ditto, there. "And I'm ready for a new challenge in my life!"

"I see." John David Honeycutt sounded skeptical. He tapped the pages of my hastily assembled resume against the gleaming desktop, and I struggled not to fidget.

So far, it seemed to be going well. I'd arrived at his campus office early, then waited half an hour for him to turn up.

"I'm sorry I'm late, Ms. Waller. Meeting ran long." He'd been speaking as he approached me down a long corridor.

I assured him that it was no problem and was secretly pleased to have him at a momentary disadvantage.

While he shifted books and folders to one arm and unlocked the office, I took a good look at this scholarly member of the fabulous Honeycutts. He was on the younger side of thirty-five, I'd say. Average height — maybe six feet. Just a bit too thin for my taste. The gray blazer he wore looked expensive — well cut and in a wonderful fabric. His khaki-colored slacks had a crease that could cut paper, and I wondered wildly if he had a personal valet or merely wielded a mean iron. He had black hair, wavy and thick, and it came down over the collar of his shirt in an artfully haphazard style.

"After you." He stepped back, letting me enter the office first, then moved around me to the big wooden desk that dominated the room. The materials he held thumped onto the desktop, joining other stacks of books and papers.

I seated myself in the only other chair in the room without waiting for him to direct me. For several moments I sat in silence as he rifled through mail and cleared a space for my resume directly in front of him.

"All right." He adjusted his tie, sat down. "All right."

Our conversation had followed the pattern of all interviews. Qualifications, references, experience. I certainly had plenty of all three, and I'd worked on my resume one full day to reflect that.

"You have a degree from this very university, I see." He rubbed his chin thoughtfully. "Art history. That could be useful, I suppose." He wasn't speaking to me then, I knew, so I just nodded my head.

After that he tuned me back in, asking that "why" question. When I gave my well-rehearsed reply, he accepted it without question, scribbling a note in the margin of the paper he held. Dropping his pencil, he sat back. His arms stretched up overhead, and I heard several vertebrae settle back into place, bringing forth a sigh of contentment from John David Honeycutt. When he smiled he revealed two very even rows of very white teeth. Almost too many teeth for one mouth, it seemed at the time to my dazzled eyes.

"Well, Gretchen," he paused. "May I call you Gretchen? Right, then. Well, Gretchen, if you want the job, it's yours." He held up one hand when I opened my mouth to accept. "I know you don't really have any clerical experience, but that should be the easy part of this job. Research skills are more essential just now. As long as you can peck out the letters on the keyboard, that should be sufficient."

My inward sigh of relief was nearly audible. That was a standard I could meet. I jumped in. "When can I start?"

"Tomorrow too soon?"

"Nope."

"Great, then. We'll have a day of orientation here, then head for Mill Hollow."

"Excuse me?"

Relaxed now, he swiveled back and forth in his chair, explaining in a casual tone, "All the family papers are in storage at Mill Hollow. That's the family estate in the north woods." Our eyes met. "I'm sure you've heard of it."

Indeed, I had. Whenever the Honeycutts were in the news, the sprawling compound was mentioned. The family summered there each year. Big reunions were held on the lawns. It had been home to at least a dozen Honeycutt nuptials over the years. And then, of course, there'd been the scandals, including the biggest one, which stretched unspoken between us now. I certainly wasn't about to bring it up and hardly expected him to. But John David Honeycutt turned out to be a man of surprises.

"I've told you I'm planning to do a book.

18

A biography on my family." He waited for my nod. His lips, wide and full, pressed together for an instant, revealing an emotional strain. "And that's true. I do plan to write the definitive work. But, also," he leaned forward, elbows on the desktop, a look of urgency in his eyes, "I plan to clear my grandfather of that murder charge."

CHAPTER THREE

There! It was out. I swallowed hard, not sure what to say or how to respond. I needn't have worried. My new employer only stopped to take a breath.

"When the murder occurred and throughout the trial, I knew my grandfather was innocent. Gretchen, he isn't a man capable of violence. He's a loving, generous, compassionate person."

I cleared my throat, ventured a query. "But the evidence —"

"Circumstantial!" The word exploded from his mouth with all the force of his belief. If strength of conviction counted for anything, Henry Hanover Honeycutt was as good as free.

"Oh, I know there's no reason for you to believe me, Gretchen. No reason anyone should. But I know what I know — what I feel!" One hand pressed against his chest. His green eyes, the color of marble, sparked with intensity and excitement. When he smiled at me, the switch from serious to cheerful came so rapidly it was startling.

I was taken aback by the mood shift and merely sat, speechless.

"We have our work cut out for us. A tough row to hoe and all those other clichés. But I'm determined to succeed."

"I'm sure you will," I told him, meaning the words.

He tipped his head to one side. "With your help."

For the space of two heartbeats our eyes held, then I chickened out, looking away into my lap and my intertwined fingers, before venturing a question. "How long do you anticipate this project taking?"

"Hmmm . . ." John let the sound fade out slowly as he reached for a calendar at the front of the desk. "Well, let's see." He flipped a few of the pages back and forth. "January, February . . ." He trailed off again. "Spring. Optimistically, I'd say spring. Will that be a problem?"

No, no, I wanted to shout. Take all the time you need. A year! Even two!

"Oh, no," I said calmly, hiding my elation at the thought of six months of steady employment. "That will be just fine."

When he brought up the subject of salary,

21

I didn't haggle. I didn't need to, the sum he quoted was more than I would have expected.

"Of course, you needn't worry about room and board. And the staff will provide meals as well."

"Staff?" The concept of servants was so foreign to me, and yet to him, naturally, it was nothing out of the ordinary.

"Yes. It's a skeletal staff during the winter. The family descends for two weeks around Christmas, and we bring in extra help for that. But, otherwise, the place is pretty quiet until Memorial Day." He paused for thought, remembering. "Summer is when Mill Hollow shines." He grinned, "We sail, we swim. We hike in the hills. It's a great place. Was a great place to be a kid."

The interview had ended, obviously, and I was glad to see such a friendly demeanor emerge. It could be quite pleasant working for this man, I decided. These next few months promised to be exciting ones. At the end of them I'd have plenty of money saved to put toward my art.

Oh, Sandy, Sandy, thank you! I thought, leaning back in my chair as John continued strolling down memory lane.

"Well don't forget to write, Gretchen."

Sandy engulfed me in a big farewell hug, her third in the last five minutes. We were standing at the curb outside my apartment building waiting for John to pick me up. Next to us on the sidewalk was a stack of mismatched luggage on loan from Sandy.

"Don't be silly." I squeezed her hard.

She was such a tiny thing, it was like hugging a bird, and I had to bend at the knees to reach her. She'd stopped growing when she hit five feet even and had never weighed more than one hundred pounds. Growing up, we'd been Mutt and Jeff, me taller and fifty pounds heavier. She'd been a tower of strength when I forced myself to diet in high school, inspiring me, coaching, being supportive. Twenty-five pounds had slowly evaporated and we'd both rejoiced when I'd been able to buy my prom dress in a size smaller than even I had hoped for.

Now I felt tears well up in my eyes and blinked them away. This was no time to be sentimental. I never had been, and now was not the time to start.

I squeezed again, then released her. "Maybe I'll even spring for a long distance call," I teased.

"Yes, do!" Her blue eyes sparked with excitement. "Take notes on everything you see. The furniture, the artwork." She smacked her lips in exaggeration. "The family photographs!"

"Sandy, I'll ask him to autograph a picture for you, okay?"

She giggled. "Oh, I know you'll have a wonderful time."

"I'll be working," it seemed necessary to remind her.

"Yes, I know," she rushed on. "But — what a place!" Her arms spread wide, illustrating the grandeur, the sprawl of Mill Hollow.

A car pulled over to the curb just in front of us, and I think we both gave a sigh of disappointment. John was at the wheel all right, but the car was not the flashy, late-model vehicle we'd both unconsciously been expecting. Oh, it was a perfectly suitable car, about five years old, in need of a wash, and painted almost the exact same green as his eyes.

When he rolled to a stop, he gave a brief toot of the horn in greeting, then popped from behind the wheel, practically crackling with excitement. "Hello, Gretchen! Glad to see you're ready." He eyed the mountain of bags at my side. "It looks like you'll be prepared for any eventuality," he teased.

His gaze shifted from the suitcases to Sandy as he stepped forward, hand extended. I hurried through the introductions, watching Sandy drink in the thrill of meeting a famed Honeycutt. She didn't exactly drop a curtsy, but I could tell she was fighting the instinct.

John certainly didn't look rich or famous this morning, dressed in jeans and a corduroy bomber jacket whose collar was frayed from daily contact with whiskers. Within the space of five minutes, he'd loaded my stuff into the car next to his own bags and hurried Sandy and me into final farewells. She was still waving as we turned the corner at the end of the block, and I swiveled around in my seat for one last glimpse.

As I settled back down, rearranging my seatbelt, John said, "She seems like a nice gal."

"Gosh, yes! She's the one who told me about this job," I told him, and he nodded.

"Ah."

He didn't respond further, and I wasn't sure how chatty I should be, so I watched out the window in silence as my neighborhood slipped by. John turned on the radio, tuned in to the national news, and kept his eyes on the road. Soon, we were on the freeway, through the downtown interchange and on the open, uncongested highway north. Only a few eighteen-wheelers shared the lanes with us.

When the headlines were repeated at the top of the hour, John stretched out a finger and changed the station to one playing country music.

"That's enough depressing news for one day, huh?" he remarked, glancing over at me.

"Yes, sure. This is fine. Better." My mind had been miles away, and it took me a few seconds to gather my thoughts.

We had been driving for just over an hour when John suggested, "Let's take a break at the next exit. My eyes are starting to cross." He suited his action to the words, and I laughed in shocked surprise at the sight.

"You know, you could get us killed that way," I scolded when he returned to normal, signaling at the exit.

"Oh, Gretchen, don't tell me you're a worry wart." He steered into the parking area of a big gas station advertising food, cold drinks and lottery tickets. "I was just funnin' ya."

We got out of the car and headed inside the station, John scoffing at my concern. "There are those who say I have an odd sense of humor, Gretchen, so expect the unexpected." He cocked one eyebrow dramatically, then swept away down an aisle of the mini-mart, leaving me to puzzle over his remark.

Shaking my head, I muttered aloud, "It's true. The rich are different!"

It got colder the further north we went, and when we neared the shores of Lake Superior a light snow began to fall. In our part of the state the grass was still visible, brown and weary-looking. Here, the countryside was covered in snow, thin in some spots, visibly deep in others. The very sight brought a smile to my face, and I took a deep, cleansing breath. It was good to be away. Away from the city. Away from the past. It was good. It was good to be so very far away.

After a truck stop lunch where the coffee had been strong and the lettuce wilted, I offered to do a stint at the wheel.

John looked startled, then pleased. "Sounds great. Just watch for the highway exit. You know where we're supposed to get off."

He'd traced our route on a map at lunch using a bright yellow highlighter. I nodded with confidence.

Adjusting his seat into its reclining position, he promptly closed his eyes.

By the time the exit appeared dusk was descending, and I flipped on the headlights.

Little clouds of snowflakes whirled across the road like ribbons in the wind, but there was no accumulation to speak of. No icy patches slowed us down. It was my own caution that kept the speedometer at fifty miles an hour.

Slowly, I pulled over onto the gravel shoulder, knowing I'd have to wake John for the next bit of directions. He'd been snoring lightly for the last twenty miles, his head turned toward the window. Deciding to let him sleep just a few minutes longer, I took the opportunity to look around me.

To the west the sky had gone purple, making the clouds look black, threatening more snow. They stood in sharp outline, lit from below, majestic, powerful, overwhelming. I took a quick breath, feeling wonder and joy, humbled by nature.

Beneath the clouds a furrowed field lay in silence. Deep grooves and high ridges marked its surface, and as I watched a rabbit darted swiftly over the terrain, disappearing near the base of a huge tree at the edge of the property. The old fence marking the boundary barely did its job, sagging and missing a few planks. Plenty of holes for the rabbit to run through, I thought.

My hands clenched the steering wheel, then released it again. I flexed my stiff fingers, wincing just a little. We'd been on the road for nearly seven hours, and I was anxious for a comfortable chair and a chance to take my boots off.

Leaning over, I gave John a poke. Gently at first, then with more force when he didn't respond. "John. John, wake up."

He groaned a little, shifting away.

I shook his shoulder. "John."

Still nothing.

Unlatching my seatbelt, I maneuvered a better grasp — both shoulders — and gave up my quiet tones.

"Mr. Honeycutt! Mr. Honeycutt!"

He gave a great start, drawing in a snort of air and scrambling to sit up. "What? Where? Wh—" he broke off, remembering where he was.

When I moved out of the way, he snapped his seat into the upright position, looking around him and blinking a few times.

"Gretchen, you should have woken me. I didn't mean to fall asleep."

"Don't worry about it. It was nice to just drive and think."

The cheek that had rested against the cushion was creased and red, imprinted with the pattern of the fabric. His hair was sleep-tousled, and he didn't make it any better when he pushed both hands through it.

A yawn escaped him before he could catch it, so I did, yawning mightily as well. We both laughed at that.

"It's not much further now," he promised. "About five miles, that way."

He pointed west, so we followed the last of the sun down the highway to the cross street, from the cross street to the private road. Up the private road, we climbed with no streetlights now to guide us. Trees pushed in on both sides of the car, dense and dark with the night.

Still at the wheel, I leaned forward and squinted, trying to see beyond the headlights.

"There's a sharp turn just ahead," John told me seconds before it appeared. "Then another and then . . . Ah, we're here." He sat back with a sigh. Of pride? Of relief?

I couldn't tell and didn't care.

Before me loomed Mill Hollow.

CHAPTER FOUR

A huge expanse of unbroken, snow-covered lawn led up to the house. Tall, towering trees stood like bookends on each side of the . . . mansion. There could be no other word for the cream-colored brick structure which rose three stories up.

I applied the brakes and counted aloud. "Six, seven, eight. There are eight chimneys on that house," I told John, who nodded.

"Right." He wasn't surprised, of course. Didn't every family's country home have eight chimneys?

I shook my head in wonder. "Well, it has fewer windows than the Chrysler building," I said smugly.

John looked confused. "What?"

"That's a quote from Philip Marlowe. The words are Raymond Chandler's, but they fit, don't you think?"

The main entrance had double doors with mullioned windows and a pediment frame.

Two wings of the house jutted forward just a bit, and the section on the western side had the added benefit of a conservatory. The wall facing us appeared to be all glass, and I shivered, picturing the heating bill.

All the windows on the second floor were framed with shutters, while the third-floor windows were dormers. The steep angle of the roof was trimmed in gingerbread, which looked like fanciful frosting on a very sturdy, traditional building.

"How old is this place, anyway?" I allowed the car to creep forward on the circular drive toward the lighted front entrance.

"Not as old as you'd think. It was built in the 1870s, but it's modeled after a house in England that's two hundred years older."

"The Honeycutt ancestors?"

"Oh, no. I wish I could say that's it, but the truth is my great-great-great," he counted the generations out on his fingers. "Grandfather had visions of grandeur."

We pulled up to the entrance. There were five steps leading to the front door. Two big stone lions perched on either side of the stairway, their left paws raised in greeting.

"If you know anything about Honeycutt history," John went on. "You'll know the family fortune came from sheep. Not very elegant. Not something I'm proud of." He paused, adding softly, "Poor sheep."

"So, you're not from landed gentry?" I clarified.

"Not at all. But old man Honeycutt wasn't going to let a little detail like that stop him from having all the trappings."

"Ah! I see!" I bit back the word I planned to use, but John said it.

"Imposter! That's what he was. A farmer in gentleman's clothing. Of course, there's nothing wrong with being working class. If you ask me, there's a lot more wrong with being upper class, but that's a whole other story."

He broke off as the big double doors opened from inside and a middle-aged couple appeared at the top of the steps, a big, dark dog standing between them. John climbed from the car and hurried forward, giving each a quick embrace, then leaning down to pat the dog's head. I looked away from the homecoming scene, taking the chance to stretch my legs and breathe in the fresh air.

It was wonderful there, so secluded and quiet. Over the drone of conversation, only the sound of the wind in the trees could be heard. I tipped my head back, looking up, up, up past the roof of the house to the clear, bright sky suspended above. Inky black and sparkling, it covered my world now.

How could I capture it on canvas, I wondered? My pen and ink could never hope to match its depth and majesty.

"Gretchen, come on over!" John waved an arm, drawing me into his circle.

With a smile in place, I stepped forward, my boots crunching over old snow. Extending a hand, I said, "Hi, I'm Gretchen Waller."

"Gretchen, these are the Crowells. Al and Mary. And this," he scratched the dog behind the ears, "is Big Nick."

Mary and Al were in their late fifties or so, and looked as if they thrived on the country air. They were about the same height, maybe five foot eight, and had acquired the softer outlines of middle age. Full cheeks and fuller bodies made them look similar in appearance, reinforcing the old belief that people eventually begin to look like their mate.

Mary smiled and the motion caused her cheeks to lift, shifting the glasses she wore. "Pleased to meet you, Gretchen. Welcome to Mill Hollow." Her voice was low, robust and deep. She was dressed casually in a plum-colored jogging suit and sneakers, and smelled faintly of good cooking.

Al's handshake was brisk. Up, down, release. Then he took a step back away from me in a way which seemed deferential or shy. Mary's skill in the kitchen had gone to his waist, the paunch straining the buttons on his plaid flannel shirt. His hair was quite thin on top but retained some of its color in that salt-and-pepper look. Mary's, by contrast, was snow white and heavy. She wore it in a bob, which seemed to emphasize the roundness of her face.

"It's a pleasure to meet you," I said sincerely. "I'm really looking forward to my work here." It couldn't hurt to throw that in.

I held out a hand to Big Nick, who had been sniffing my boots. Big Nick was almost the size of a German shepherd, with short, dark fur and liquid brown eyes.

His wet nose touched my palm in acceptance. "Gorgeous dog," I said.

John dropped to his knees and rubbed the big dog's head. "Oh, yes. He's a gem. Just a mutt, you know, but the best dog in the world."

"Oh, you'll spoil him with all that sweet talk," Mary warned.

"I'll get your bags, miss," Al offered. "You all go on in and have something to eat. There's soup and a casserole." Even as he spoke, he was heading down the steps to the car, and Mary was herding John and me inside, Big Nick at our heels.

John slipped his arm companionably around Mary's waist, and she gave him a squeeze. "It's so good to see you," I heard her say quietly.

I trailed behind at what seemed a respectable distance, not wanting to eavesdrop. Once we were through the front door an even bigger gap developed as they moved on, and I dawdled, gaping.

The place had the proportions of a museum but held evidence of homey touches. A cathedral ceiling soared overhead. Ancestral portraits graced the walls, mixing easily with more contemporary photographs. A magnificent hat stand — marble and framing an elaborately carved mirror — stood near the entrance. A few hand-knit scarves and woolly hats dangled from it now. On the floor some rubber boots looked like they had taken up permanent residency.

Beneath my feet, the tile floor stretched nearly to the vanishing point, eventually leading out to the back lawn. A bold black and white check, it gleamed under soft lights. How long did it take Mary to wax it, I wondered.

Wandering off to one wall, I saw an array

of framed photographs on a long, narrow table. Glancing over the display, I could see these were more recent than those on the walls. There were family groups, action shots and candid scenes, just like those of families everywhere. Recognizing John's broad smile, I lifted one frame from behind a few others. There was my new boss, grinning widely as he cannonballed into a swimming pool.

"Here, now! I don't think you should be looking at that!"

CHAPTER FIVE

With a start, I whirled around, my cheeks flaming with guilt. Caught in the act!

But John was smiling, reaching to take the picture from me and give it a closer inspection. "That was a great day," he recalled, setting it back into place. "Fourth of July. Hotter than — well, pretty hot. Too bad it's not summer, Gretchen, or you could try out the pool. Do you swim?"

His chatter gave me a chance to collect myself. "Yes, actually. I do. I used to teach a life-saving course, in fact. Every summer, all through college."

John nodded, as if pleased. "Well, maybe we can squeeze in some ice skating for R and R instead. I think there are about fifty pairs of skates in the basement."

Turning, he placed one hand gently on my elbow and guided me down the long hallway toward the back of the house. We passed a very stately looking stairway that ran along one wall, curving upward in a graceful twist of wood. Doors opened off the main hall on either side, but most of them were closed now, so I had no idea what rooms lay beyond. I imagined a library, a drawing room and perhaps a music room as well.

All mental wandering ended when we finally arrived at the kitchen. The smell of good food made my stomach rumble, and I realized that it had been several hours since we'd last stopped for a snack.

"Mmm. Something smells wonderful," I said, smiling at Mary, who stood near a huge, state-of-the-art oven.

She was stirring something in a tall silver kettle and said over her shoulder, "You two make yourselves comfortable. I'll have things ready in a jiffy."

John needed no further prompting. "We'll sit here with you," he told her, leading the way to a huge square farm table set in the middle of the room. He pulled out a chair for me, adding, "That way, you can fill us in on all the news."

"Oh," Mary scoffed. "Not much news to tell, Johnny. The Harrises are off to the West for a month or two. The county budget for snow plowing has been cut, and we've been having a bit of trouble with the satellite television. That's about it."

She thumped two ceramic bowls in front of us and set a basket filled with homemade bread in the space between us. Steam rising from the bowl carried the fragrant smell of thick vegetable stew, and I was quick to dip my spoon.

After pouring coffee into four cups Mary joined us at the table, nibbling on ginger cookies and chatting amicably with John about local events. When Al arrived, he moved straight to the coffee pot, refilling our cups before warming up his own and easing into his chair. He looked across at me and winked as if he knew how I felt. The gesture made me relax as some of that fifth wheel sense went away. As soon as there was a break in the conversation he jumped in, changing it to something more immediate.

"So, you're finally going to do that book, John?"

"Yes. Do the book and clear Gramp's name."

Al lifted his cup and sipped noisily. "Tall order, son. Don't you think that hotsy-tots lawyer would have done that if it were possible?"

John didn't answer the question. "Are you saying you think he did it? You think my grandfather is a murderer?" Anger flared beneath his words and behind his eyes.

There was a long, tense silence. The spoon felt frozen in my hand, and I wished I were anywhere else. Mary shifted nervously as the two men exchanged looks. At last, Al spoke quietly. "You know no one was more surprised than me when all that happened. I never thought he was a man capable of that. Didn't I say so often enough?"

"So, when did you change your mind?" John's voice was acidic.

"It's not that. It's more like . . ." He shrugged big shoulders in a gesture of defeat. "The world isn't fair. There's no such thing as justice."

"And you can't fight city hall?" John's fist hit the tabletop, making the spoons clatter and jump. "I can't believe you think we should just let Gramps sit in prison. That's a crime. The real crime!" His nostrils widened and tense lines etched his features.

From where he was stretched out on a rug in front of the sink, I saw Big Nick's ears twitch at the raised voice. His eyes darted over to us humans, assessing the situation.

Mary took a deep breath, straightening up. "You just hold on a minute there, John, and stop talking before you say something you'll regret." Her eyes flashed briefly in my

41

direction, reminding John he had an audience. "Al and I would do anything possible to help your grandpa, and you know it. Frankly," she shrugged. "I wish you the best. Henry is not a strong man. He won't last long in jail. I'm surprised he's held on this long, if you want the truth. But when you get as old as we are, you see the world a little different. You don't believe in happy endings and the American way anymore."

"Just can't," Al put in, shaking his head.

"Try as we might," Mary went on. She stood up, leaning over the table to pat John's hand. "But we'll help you. Please know that. We'll do what that lawyer couldn't, Johnny."

"Could be dangerous," Al spoke again, soberly.

"How so?" John's voice still held a challenge, but his anger had tempered.

"Well, use your head. If your grandpa didn't do it, someone else did. Someone else who isn't in jail," he paused, but just for an instant. "Someone who doesn't want to be in jail."

"So, you're saying the real murderer might come looking for me?"

Al took another drink from his mug. He looked down into the cup as he spoke. "Makes sense to me."

"To me, too," I spoke without thinking. The words just popped out and took us all by surprise. I'd been sitting so quietly, feeling like an eavesdropper. And yet, it would have made more of a stir to excuse myself from the room. So I listened — and added my two cents.

All three of them turned to look at me, making me feel like an animal on display at the zoo. I fidgeted, spinning my spoon in a circle on the tabletop as I looked from one to the other. Shrugging, I said, "If a person's committed one murder, the next one might be easier. I don't know." Another shrug.

John's green eyes clouded as his forehead furrowed in thought. Perhaps he gave our views consideration, but in the end he just shook his head. "I have to try. I just have to! I owe it to Gramps." He sighed heavily.

Mary pushed back her chair, moving stiffly, as if her ankles hurt. "I say, let's leave all this for now. It's late. You two must be exhausted after that long drive. Why don't you call it a night and get a fresh start in the morning?"

Her suggestion sounded good to me. My eyelids were drooping, and the beginning of a headache felt dull in the back of my skull. Leaving the men behind, Mary and I left the kitchen, walking side by side down the long corridor and up the staircase. We made small talk, but not much of it. I let the surroundings slide by unobserved, thinking only of a warm bath and a long nap.

We turned left at the top of the stairs, went what seemed like half a mile, then turned left again. This wing apparently housed the bedrooms. Mary stopped at a door that looked exactly like all the others, and I wondered briefly how I'd ever find it again. A trail of bread crumbs would work nicely.

She switched on the light. "Here you go, Gretchen. The bathroom is just across the hallway. Breakfast is in the dining room, anytime between seven and nine, so you just sleep as long as you'd like. I don't think John will expect you to be on the job first thing." She stepped aside so I could enter the room. "G'night."

Her footsteps faded away down the hall. I closed the heavy wooden door, leaning against it for a moment to let out the yawn I'd been holding back. Suddenly even the thought of fishing through my suitcase for pajamas seemed like too much work. Flopping onto the high, fluffy mattress, I fell instantly asleep.

CHAPTER SIX

"So, tell me what you know about my grandfather," John suggested over toast and jam the next morning.

We were in the wood-paneled dining room, eating off fine china and drinking our coffee from delicate cups. The goblet containing my orange juice was surely crystal. It was heavy and substantial in my hand.

John's question wasn't totally unexpected. We'd been discussing the project and my role in it. Talking about the Honeycutt family history had led to a verbal dance around the Honeycutt family scandals.

I buttered another slice of toast before answering. "I just know what everyone knows. He was raised to continue building on the family fortune. Went to law school and married a wealthy and beautiful woman. He tried to clean up the family image, eager to make the Honeycutt name respectable."

"Respectable and important, not just wealthy," John put in.

"Yes. So, the sons went to law school, and the daughters married well."

"Very well."

"But there were always scandals plaguing the family, anyway. Bootlegging, mafia ties," I hesitated wondering how much of this litany John wanted to hear.

He nodded to prod me.

"Then, two years ago," I cleared my throat, spreading the jam around my toast a few more times. "A man was found dead. Murdered. They said your grandfather did it."

"Yes. A man in his late seventies attacked and killed an intruder here on the grounds. Delivered a blow to the back of the head, then strangled the stranger with his bare, arthritic hands." John rolled his eyes at such logic. "It's incredible anyone ever believed it."

I played my assigned role of devil's advocate. "But there was evidence. Your grandfather had no alibi. Said he'd been out walking with the dog. And he was — is — a big man. Known to have mixed it up with people in the past. Violent temper."

"He hit a photographer once," John clarified. "Twenty years ago."

46

"Then it turned out the dead guy wasn't a stranger. He was connected to one of your grandfather's tangential business ventures. One of the questionable ones."

"You'd think the cops would have been glad he was dead," John muttered.

"So, with that connection —"

"That tenuous connection!"

"The jury convicted, and he's doing life behind bars." The conclusion to the story came quickly. I wanted to get it over with, knowing how painful it must be to hear and relive.

"Not if I can help it, Gretchen." John's resolve was unshaken. He gulped his juice and pushed away from the table. "When you've finished with breakfast, meet me in the library." At my distressed look, he gave directions. "Opposite side of this hall, four doors down. We can get started this morning!" His smile was friendly, cheerful and eager.

I returned it in full, raising my glass in a toast. "Looking forward to it!"

By noon, I wasn't so sure.

John was a perfectionist. Energetic and with high standards of productivity, he whirled around me, sweeping me along with talk of game plans, deadlines and areas of inquiry. My head ached with the sheer volume of information and procedures I was expected to learn.

Eventually, I held up both hands. "Uncle, uncle! You said I didn't need to know much about computers. You said I didn't even need to know how to type!" I eyed the laptop computer on the desk in front of me as if it were an alien life form. Truly, it was to me. Starving artists can't afford luxuries like laptops and wireless internet access. I navigate the internet from the public library — and then only when I absolutely have to. As for real typing, well, one word processing class at the community college hovered in my distant past, but you know what they say: use it or lose it. I had lost it long ago.

One eyebrow arched high on John's face, and he rolled up the sleeves of his shirt as he talked. "Well, Gretchen, just the rudimentary stuff. An afternoon with an instruction manual will give you all the help you need. Then, just enter these files I've already compiled." One hand patted a foot-high stack of papers covered in indecipherable handwriting.

"And what are they, again?"

He'd told me the contents somewhere along the line, but I'd forgotten. I rubbed my temples with both hands.

"Easily accessible, verifiable history. Birth and death dates. Marriages, divorces. You know, the ordinary stuff."

"Got it." I wrote "ordinary stuff" on a piece of scrap paper and taped it to the top of the pile.

A shadow of doubt crossed John's face as he watched me. "Would you say you're an organized person, Gretchen?"

I flinched at his tone. Was he going to be my mother now, telling me to clean my room? Straightening up, I clenched my jaw so tight the words could barely squeeze out. "I'm very organized. In my own way."

"Method to your madness?"

"Yes. Just as I'm sure there is to yours," I said.

He didn't seem offput by my remark, especially after looking around the room at the disorder he'd created in a single morning. One hand came up to rub at his jawbone. "Point taken." Slowly, he surveyed our spacious surroundings, his hands braced on slim hips encased in well-worn denim. When he turned back to me, he grinned. "It would seem I work best when engulfed in chaos."

A chaotic perfectionist, I thought, biting my lip and feeling a certain queasiness. Ah, well. In for a penny . . .

"Why don't you give me some time with the instruction manual?" I suggested. I flapped the bright yellow **WORD FOR DUMMIES** book in my hand. "I'm a quick learner. By the end of the day, I'll have a good start." My words were optimistic and, from the look on his face, he knew it.

"Sure enough, Gretchen. I'll be over here." At the big table near huge double windows he had set up a command post of sorts. How he'd be able to concentrate with that fabulous view of the snow-covered garden and the woods beyond, I couldn't imagine.

With a sigh I swiveled my chair around, away from tempting views and other man-made distractions.

"Chapter one, page one." Ugh.

We took an hour for lunch in the early afternoon. I ate quickly, then asked permission to take a walk around the estate. The central heating and technical prose were making me sleepy. A little fresh air and exercise were just what I needed.

To my surprise, John hesitated. "Where do you plan to go?" he asked. "Mill Hollow covers a lot of ground."

I shrugged. "I'll stick close by. Just around

the house itself."

"Yes. All right, but don't be too long."

I was already pushing back my chair. "Maybe you can give me the grand tour someday. I'd love to see the place."

John's lips pursed. "Yes. We'll do that. Soon," he promised.

As I donned coat and gloves, I puzzled over my new boss. What a contradictory man he was! Easy-going and open one minute, stern taskmaster the next. Where did I plan to go! Did he think I'd be gone all afternoon? Did he think I'd wander into the woods and get lost?

The heavy front door closed with a thud behind me, and I scurried down the steps at a rapid rate. I turned left at the bottom of the steps, moving with big, arm-swinging strides past the windows and around the corner of the mansion. It was cold, but the sun was out, and there was no wind. My breath came in little clouds as I chugged along. With every step the blinking cursor on the computer screen faded away, and the image of John's puzzled face vanished with a poof.

It was lovely here, no doubting that. And, by the look of the snow, I wasn't the first person to pass this way. A single set of footprints marred the pristine surface, stretching the length of the building and continuing to the vanishing point. Just for fun I put my foot into one of the deeper prints. There was ample space around it. The walker had been a man. Al, I decided at once, patrolling the grounds.

Without conscious thought I followed the trail, crunching happily over the frozen surface and sniffling with the cold. Beyond the conservatory, past what would be formal gardens come the thaw, across the huge expanse of lawn and into the woods.

Oh, it was so quiet here! Just the sound of my feet on the snow and my breath, raspy now with the unusual exertion. Lost in thought, I jumped and froze when the harsh call of a crow broke the stillness. I craned my neck, searching the canopy of trees. There he was, a stark black outline perched high on a thin branch. It was a wonder the spindly surface supported his weight. As I watched, he called again, and this time the sound didn't jar or startle. This time, it was like music. A chill ran through me, up my spine and across my scalp, and I shivered with the sheer pleasure of this place. Out of doors, as free as that bird . . .

Well, perhaps not.

Reluctantly, I pushed back my sleeve to check my watch. As I'd feared, too much time had passed. If I didn't hurry, I'd be late.

Just one more deep breath, I promised myself. Just one more moment of intense peace.

But it was not to be.

As I stood with the silence pressing down all around me, I heard the unmistakable sound of a footstep in the forest. Someone born and bred in the country wouldn't give the noise a thought, I knew. It must be a deer. Or a sizeable raccoon. Or some other form of wildlife. Maybe a bear?

By the time a vision of a big black bear crossed my mind I was moving. I went back the way I had come, swallowing down a bubble of something that could easily have turned to fear. I wasn't running, just walking quickly, fighting the urge to sprint. Eventually, the trees gave way to the clear, open spaces of the lawn and gardens.

Slowing my pace to something more reasonable, I felt silly for getting spooked. I laughed out loud as I neared the house. What would the others think if they'd seen me? It was probably just a squirrel, I thought. I'd been scampering away from a squirrel.

My nose was cold now, and my cheeks were prickling. The thought of the indoors didn't seem stifling anymore. And a cup of hot chocolate would go down pretty easy, too. I'd have to stop in the kitchen before heading back to the library . . .

Rounding the corner of the house at a clip, I collided heavily with an immovable object. The force of the impact knocked the breath from my lungs, and I jumped back, expecting to see that bear from the woods.

"You okay, Gretchen?"

It was Al. Big, overstuffed Al, looking rather like a bear in a bulky winter jacket trimmed with something fuzzy. The hood pulled up over his head acted like a periscope, surrounding his face to block the cold. In his hands, he held a hammer. When I glanced down, I saw his toolbox and a few tools spread out at the base of a storm window.

My hand to my chest, I laughed at myself. "Yes, I'm fine. Oh, you gave me a scare! I hope I didn't hurt you."

He shook his head. "I think I'd do you more damage than you'd do me." He patted his tummy and smiled.

"Thankless job you have today." I indicated the repair project.

Al scoffed. "Won't take long, at least, once I get at it."

The subtle hint wasn't lost on me. "I'll

see you later, then." I took a step past him as he knelt to begin work. His footprints were clearly visible in the snow and, quickly, curiously, I slipped my foot into one. The depression was bigger than my boot, as I'd expected, but not nearly as big as the print I'd seen earlier.

I frowned. Who else had been out walking on the estate? Who else had circled so close to the house, then headed deep into the woods?

I remembered the sound in the forest I had attributed to wildlife, and my eyes widened. Someone had been nearby, hidden by the trees! Watching? Lurking? I took to my heels.

CHAPTER SEVEN

"Well, I'd dock your paycheck for getting back late, except I see you've come bearing gifts."

John was sprawled in an armchair pulled up close to the fireplace that dominated one wall of the library. Beside him was a stack of notecards, proof that he hadn't been dawdling in my absence.

Setting down the tray I carried, I passed him a cup of hot chocolate filled to the brim. He took it with both hands, carefully sipping.

"Your idea?" He indicated the treat.

I nodded. "Yes. That walk was refreshing — but cold! This should take the chill off, though." I drank from my own mug before adding, "Then I'll get right back to work."

"So, what did you think of the place?" he asked after a moment. "It's quite a hike around the perimeter."

"Oh, I didn't make it all that way! Just

along the back and a little bit into the woods." I detailed my journey.

"Sounds good. Maybe I should have come with you. A little exercise would have worked off that lunch." He didn't sound convincing.

"Next time," I suggested with a grin.

"Yes. Next time."

I thought for a moment, choosing my next words carefully. "Does anyone else live on the estate, John? Who is the nearest neighbor?"

He answered the last question first. "The Harris family lives about half a mile west of here. I guess you could call them neighbors. Of course, I don't know any of them very well. Haven't had much contact through the years."

I digested this tidbit of information, waiting.

"As for the estate, there's a cottage back in the forest where the gamekeeper lived in the old days. When we were kids, we played there in the summertime. Once in a while, our grandparents let us sleep there overnight." He chuckled at the memory. "That was an adventure. I'm surprised the place is still standing!"

"But," I pressed the point. "No one lives there now? You're sure about that?"

John set his cup down on the table beside him and sat up a little straighter. He looked openly curious, eyes wide, lips pressed together. The toes of one foot tapped the rug, I noticed, as if he were anxious. "It's been empty for years, Gretchen," he told me. His tone challenged me to prove otherwise. "Why are you asking? Did you see someone? I can have Al take a look around. We've never had much trouble with hunters. All the land is clearly posted —"

"No, no," I cut him off. "I didn't see anyone. I just —" I shrugged. "I thought I heard something, and there was another set of footprints in the snow." Said aloud, the specifics didn't amount to much.

John's foot stopped tapping, and I noticed for the first time that his feet were big. His dingy old sneakers could have belonged to the NBA. Or so it seemed. But were his feet big enough to make those tracks? If so, he'd simply tell me that now. Tell me of an early morning jaunt across the snow.

Instead, he leaned forward, hands on his knees. "What did you hear?"

I described the sound, brushing the incident off. "It was probably nothing. I guess I'm just not used to the great outdoors." Really, I was sorry I'd even mentioned it when I saw the look on John's face deepen

58

from casual interest to genuine concern.

"I'm glad you told me this, Gretchen. I'll speak to Al. Maybe he and I can go check out the cottage. It's possible someone's taken up residence there. A vagrant. A poacher."

"Better safe than sorry." The old cliché seemed apt.

I drained the last of my chocolate, then headed across the room to my workstation. When I looked back over my shoulder at John he was still sitting in the same spot, deep in thought.

Soon, the only sound to fill the room was the click of the computer keys as I tentatively began the data entry. It was tedious work at first until I developed a rhythm. Soon, to my surprise, I was picking up speed and getting a great sense of satisfaction each time I hit the "enter" button. Every now and then I'd be forced to pause and ponder whether the squiggle written on John's page of notes was an "e" or an "i," but even that became easier as the hours passed.

When my crabbed hands began to ache, I took a break. Wiggling my fingers and grimacing, I slipped quietly from the room. It was easy to find the well-appointed powder room. It was directly across from the kitchen. The first time I'd been in it, I'd spent a good five minutes just looking around.

The big sink was marble, the color of a seashell, and it stood on two elaborately detailed brass legs. A huge mirror hung above it, its edges outlined in mother-of-pearl. The glass itself was just wavy enough to make me blink. The wallpaper had a creamy background, a flocked design stood out to the touch. Frosted glass at the window was the only concession made to modern times, and I wondered irrelevantly if the original glass had been broken during a baseball game on the lawn.

As I stepped out of the room I could hear voices from the kitchen and smell dinner being prepared. I would have kept right on walking except I heard my name. My ears pricked up, and I stopped in my tracks.

"— just don't know how smart it is to be bringing other people into all this." Al's low tone carried easily.

Into all what?

"I know, dear. Especially now. It seemed particularly ill-timed, but there was no way for John to know that."

"Foolhardy! Just foolhardy! No good will come of it."

"But what if he can prove Henry's in-

60

nocence?" Mary sounded hopeful. "Surely that would be good."

I heard a chair scrape backward, then Al spoke, sounding angry. "You had better think about what you just said, Mary. Think long and hard about whether you want the murderer's name revealed, because you might not like the answer."

"Oh, Al, honestly! You and your theories don't scare me." She paused, and I could picture her wagging her finger when she went on. "And you better watch what you say, or someone will sue you for slander."

My mind whirled, processing this fascinating information. I bit my lip and tipped my head to make sure I caught every word.

"All I know is, I never saw anything. I never heard anything, and nobody can say I did!" Al said, sounding as if he'd said it a hundred times before.

His voice seemed closer now, and my heart gave a leap. It wouldn't do to be caught snooping. Silently, I spun on my heel and slipped back into the powder room. Standing up against the door, I pressed my palms flat against the wood. Al's heavy footsteps moved past me, down the hallway. The door onto the back lawn creaked open, then shut with a bit more force than necessary. For a few seconds longer I stayed where I was, turning over the exchange I'd just heard.

Obviously Al knew something — or thought he did — about the murder and the killer's identity. Something important enough for him to take a vow of silence, and for him to let an old man sit in jail.

What, I wondered, could be more important than justice?

I frowned, then caught my reflection in the mirror and stopped. I had only been hired to be the secretary and do the odd bit of research. That didn't mean I should turn into a modern-day Sherlock Holmes. But it was difficult to turn away from such intrigue. My natural curiosity had gotten me into trouble more times than I could recall, and I couldn't stand to lose another job.

Pulling open the door, I walked into the deserted hallway and headed back to the library. Even as I promised myself not to go above and beyond the call of duty, an inner bit of me determined to find out what Al knew. How awful could it be?

CHAPTER EIGHT

Later that day after dinner was over and darkness had fallen, I sat on the fluffy bed in my beautiful bedroom with a sketchpad on my lap. With swift, light strokes, I drew in the branches of the trees I had seen on my walk. The trunks were many lines, to show texture and strength. On the table at my side, the radio on the tape player I'd brought from home played softly, providing a soothing background to my labors.

All afternoon as I'd tapped away on the computer keys, I'd replayed the conversation of Al and Mary, then created scenarios to fit the words. They got more and more fanciful as time went on and, finally I'd reined in my imagination. I had no facts, so I could draw no conclusions.

Pressing my lips together, I hummed along with the tune of the moment and added a squirrel's nest to the tree in my drawing. It was more difficult to capture the look of the lowering sky and the glint of the snow. Without thinking, I scritched those mystery footprints into the picture.

Had John talked to Al yet? Had Al gone to the little cottage in the woods?

Beyond the windows, I heard the wind pick up, rattling the old frame. A fine dust of snow made a hiss against the glass, and I curled up my toes, feeling lucky to be somewhere warm and safe on such a cold night. Setting the sketchpad aside, I slipped from the bed. At the window I lifted the filmy lace curtain, looking down on the unbroken snow. If someone was staying in the little cottage they were in for a chilly night's sleep, I thought. Unless they built a fire. I scanned the treetops for telltale smoke, but saw none.

The wind gusted again with such force I took a step back. Trees bent beneath its power. Snow blew sideways. A huge cloud of the stuff came from above, off the roof, obliterating the view.

A puff of cold air touched the back of my neck.

Lifting my shoulders I shrugged it away, then stopped. I was facing the window. Why had the air been at my back? My muscles tensed. The bedroom door was firmly closed. I hadn't heard it open.

"Well, it is an old house," I said aloud, just to hear my voice.

Slowly, I let the curtain drop back into place, then worked the cord at the side of the window that drew heavy red velvet drapery over the lace panels. Only then did I turn around. The bedroom door was still closed. I could feel no draft when I held my hands near the jamb. No cold air blew in from the hallway, and yet I'd felt it, unmistakably.

The radio switched to something upbeat and snappy. I turned up the volume and then decided to go on a circle tour to find that draft. Beginning at the door I moved slowly over the faded oriental rugs that overlapped each other on the floor. This room was big, but not overly so. The decorations were elegant, made homey by their age. One wall had been papered in a floral pattern, red roses on a tea-stained background. The armoire was taller than I was, its rich cherry wood blending perfectly with the heavy dresser and vanity. A big oil landscape hung near the window. Smaller portraits dotted the other walls. Beside the bed, a little table held a lamp, a bud vase with one hot house flower and my tape player. The shelf beneath was stacked with books I had yet to examine.

Feeling silly, I opened both doors on the armoire, pushing my clothing aside to reveal its back wall. Nope, no draft coming from here. After another ten minutes of fruitless searching I gave up.

Back on the bed I retrieved my sketchpad, pulling the pencil from its resting place behind my ear. With my knees drawn up and pillows propped behind me I worked, a bit more distracted now. It was while I was hunched over drawing in a few more details, that the draft came again on the back of my neck as if someone was blowing a thin column of air across my skin. But the wall was behind me!

Jerking around, I confronted the pillows and the headboard. No breeze touched my face. Whatever had caused the breath of air had stopped. My heart pounded with an emotion I refused to identify. My stomach felt achy and bottomless. Closing my eyes, I took a deep, controlled breath.

"Get a grip, gal!" I ordered. "You've just seen too many scary old movies." I tried to smile, to resume my work, but the pencil shook in my hand. "Drat!" I tossed the pad aside, rubbed my hands over my eyes and sighed. "Drat!"

The next morning, I clicked on the computer with some degree of confidence. Yesterday's labors had gone well. I'd carefully saved the information. Now, I'd boot it up. The phrase made me laugh, made me picture applying my boot to someone's backside. I hit the appropriate keys and tapped "enter."

Nothing.

Well, I'd probably done something wrong, I decided, reaching for the instruction manual. Step by step, I did as I was shown by the line drawings and simple text. Then, "enter." Nothing.

I furrowed my brow, feeling my patience ebb. My finger came down hard on the offending key, and I smacked it several times in quick succession.

"Come on, come on!" I urged the machine. Still, the computer found no file.

John looked up at my groan of frustration. "Trouble?"

"Yes, darn, it!" I explained my problem.

"Hmm." He set down the yellow legal pad he'd been writing on and crossed the room. "Let me take a look, Gretchen."

"Gladly." I relinquished my seat and stood looking over his shoulder as he did just what I had done. It was gratifying to see him have the same results. I threw up my hands. "See? What's wrong with it?"

John leaned closer to the screen where the cursor blinked with maddening regularity. "Are you sure you saved the file?"

Without looking at him, I said too slowly, "Of course I'm sure I saved the file!" Really, it was too much. How stupid did he think I was?

"Okay, okay. Keep your shirt on. I'm just trying to weed out problems."

He fiddled and weeded another ten minutes or so. All the while, I could feel my heart slipping into my shoes, and my head started to ache with a dull, insistent pain. I knew what the diagnosis would be, knew how much work lay ahead.

John sat back, defeated. When he looked up at me, his eyes held an apology.

I shut my eyes to block out his words.

"I'm sorry, Gretchen, but it appears the file is gone. Either it wasn't saved or it's been deleted."

"I know I saved it, John. I swear!" My fist came down on the back of his chair to emphasize my point.

"Then, someone deleted it." He said the words, but I could tell he didn't believe them.

Someone deleted it. Yes, someone had. I knew it was the only solution. Remembering Al's fear over John's investigation, I felt certain he was the culprit.

"Thanks a lot, Al," I muttered under my breath.

John stood, held the chair out for me. "You'll have to begin again. Save it on the C-drive, this time."

"I'd better get started." The smile I gave him was weak, but it was the best I could manage. At the end of this day's work I vowed I'd do that C-drive thing, but I'd also back up the information on a disk and sleep with it under my pillow!

CHAPTER NINE

Al and Mary joined us for lunch that day at John's invitation. The food was hearty, perfect for winter, and delicious as always. I didn't contribute much to the conversation. Al sat directly across from me, and I couldn't help watching him. His large, calloused hands buttered a thick slice of fluffy bread, and several times he didn't wait to swallow before adding his two cents to the discussion.

"Did you erase my file?" I wanted to ask. Instead, when there was a lag, I put an amused lilt in my voice and said in an offhand way, "Boy, that computer really got the best of me this morning. Didn't it, John?"

He merely nodded, chewing.

"Why, what happened?" Mary's curiosity seemed genuine, and her sympathy did too when I explained my problem.

Al grew suddenly absorbed in his casserole, looking down, poking with his fork. Did I imagine a ruddy blush spreading up his neck?

"You know, I've had that happen to me," Mary said.

"You have?"

I must have sounded incredulous because she laughed before answering. "Yes. Even us old fogies are computer-literate these days. I keep all my recipes on file that way. Someday, I'm going to write a cookbook."

"Someday." Al's echo was skeptical.

Mary spared him a glance. "I will too. You'll see."

"Do you use the computer in the library?" I asked, adding innocently, "Maybe you can figure out what went wrong."

"Our computer is the same model, but we keep it in our rooms," Mary explained. "We have a suite just down the hallway here at the back of the house. I'll give you a tour, hmm?"

"Oh, yes. I'd like that," I said, reaching for another slice of bread.

So, Mary and Al had their own computer. Then, Al would certainly know how to access a file — and eliminate it. When I looked across the table at the top of his head, I mentally convicted him. Guilty as charged.

"By the way, Al," John said, "have you had

a chance to look into the cottage like I asked? If not, I thought perhaps Gretchen and I could take a walk, stop along the way —"

John's eyes met mine, and I nodded, but Al prevented further conversation.

"Plan to do it directly after lunch, John. Can't say I expect to find anything, though."

He glanced up at me, his eyes dark with accusation. It was startling to see, and I wondered just how John had related my story. I arched my eyebrows and said nothing.

"Well, let me know, okay?" John dismissed the issue, turning to me. "But we'll still take that walk later."

"Sounds good!"

And so it was. After another tedious stretch at the computer, going over old ground and re-entering all the things I'd done the previous day, John and I donned heavy winter clothes and tramped out the back door into the snow, Big Nick scouting the way. John's cap, a loud black-and-white checked flannel job, had flaps to cover his ears. I relied on fuzzy red earmuffs to do the job.

"Which way?" I asked, turning in a slow circle on the open lawn.

There was less than an hour of daylight

remaining. No trace of last evening's blustery winds existed, but the evidence of its passing was everywhere.

Heavy drifts of pure white snow lay in a ridge across the yard. In spots, it looked a good three feet deep, and I was glad my boots came up to my knees. Big Nick raced across the lawn, nose down, turning on a dime when John whistled him over.

My boss pointed north, into the woods directly behind the house. "You went west yesterday, right?" he asked.

"Right."

"Then, we'll go this way." He smiled down at me, looking like the child I had seen in those family photographs. "I want to show you my favorite spot on the estate."

The big old dog charged forward, his tail like a flag behind him. Apparently, he was privy to secret places too.

John was several steps in front of me, sure of his destination. I hurried to catch up. The ground was uneven beneath my feet, and the snow squeaked and scrunched as I crossed it.

"Where are we heading?" I asked. "Why is it your favorite place?" I was beside him now, glancing over to catch his expression.

He didn't look at me, but kept plodding

ahead through heavy drifts as he answered. "We're going to the pond. It's not very big and not very deep. But it's really secluded. Buried back here, actually."

I cringed inwardly at his word choice and had a moment's sensation of doubt. I hardly knew John although what I knew, I liked. There had been a murder here at his summer home, and there seemed a chance the murderer hadn't been captured. How smart was it to venture this far into these dark woods? How safe was it?

"I think you'll see what makes it special," he said, puffing only slightly from the exertion.

I took a deep breath of the icy air and nodded. We'll see soon enough, I thought.

It was at least ten minutes before the trees began to thin and a clearing emerged. And in the clearing, ringed by bushes, silent and still, was the pond. We stopped where we stood just outside the trees, taking in the almost magical scene before us.

The frozen surface of the water was silvered like a mirror and just as unbroken. The last of the sunlight made the ice shine, diamond bright and tempting. My toes itched just looking at it. Why hadn't John suggested we bring our skates?

"Oh, for a pair of skates!" I crowed, rub-

bing my mittened hands together in anticipation.

John laughed at my enthusiasm, then
reined it in. "We should check it out first,
though. To be sure it's safe. It was a warm
autumn, so it hasn't been freezing that
long."

Thinking over how cold and gloomy the
days had been in recent times, I said, "Oh,
no?"

"I mean, relatively."

"Let's check, then." I took a step forward
but stopped when John placed a hand on
my arm.

"Just a few moments more," he said, and
I knew he wanted to simply soak up the
silence, the serenity.

It wasn't a bad idea, so I joined in, tipping
my head back to watch the sky. It had been
gray, a clean, slate gray with just a hint o'
sunlight behind clouds. Now, as dusk too'
a firm hold, that gray deepened to midnig'
blue.

As I watched, snowflakes began to f;
mere specks at first, then looming big;
three dimensional as they drifted dow;
my face. One landed at the very tip o'
nose, making me giggle. Really, it
wonderful here. I felt free from car'
concern, from the problems of the pa

the mysteries of the present. Holding my arms out to the side, I stuck out my tongue, playing the children's game of catch-the-snowflake.

Beside me, I heard John laugh and urged him, "Try it! C'mon!"

He hesitated at first, probably not wanting to appear as silly as me. I gave him a teasing poke in the ribs. Any man who did cannonballs into the swimming pool shouldn't stand on ceremony when it came to goofy games, after all.

"Oh, all right." He grinned and the edges of his eyes crinkled up. The spark I'd first beheld in those eyes glinted out at me. I grinned back, then stuck my tongue out again and raced around the clearing, pursuing the delicate snowflakes.

Barking in surprise, Big Nick kept pace with me, darting off, then skidding back, sending a wave of snow up in his wake.

John did me one better, leaping into the air, mouth open, arms flailing. What a sight! I started to laugh at the undignified display, and it felt as if something inside me let loose. The dam just broke.

Once I'd begun to chuckle, I couldn't stop. When John paused in his leaping to ask innocently, "What's so funny?" I doubled over. Tears filled my eyes, and I

pressed both hands to my cheeks where the muscles were beginning to pinch.

John bounded across the space which separated us until he was suddenly so very close to me. His mittened hands reached up to cover my own. "So, I'm that funny looking, huh? Well, you are quite a sight, too, you know."

I knew all right. Imagining it, I caught my breath for the next round of giggles. The sound hung in the air, echoing in the quiet space and probably scaring off all the wildlife.

"I probably shouldn't say this," John began, his hands tightening around my fingers, "but you're cute when you laugh."

The words were surprising and unexpected. I inhaled sharply, not certain how to respond. "Well, so are you."

In unison, we moved closer. Then, quickly, before we could think about it and stop ourselves, we kissed. It was a fleeting kiss, like a very first kiss after the junior high dance. Feather light and over so swiftly it might never have happened.

I blinked. John blinked. We tried again, a bit slower this time. His lips were soft, but cool from the winter air. I pressed my lips against his, tentatively at first, then with more confidence as his hands left my cheeks to circle my waist. My heart beat heavily in my chest at this sudden turn of events, at my own pleased reaction to John's embrace.

It had been so long, so very long, since I'd allowed myself to let go, to feel, to hope. I'd been through a particularly painful breakup a while ago, one that had not been my idea. For a while, I'd been afraid I'd never feel this way again — that I'd forgotten how! But now, in John's arms, I knew that wasn't true. It was like riding a bike. Broken hearts scabbed over, given enough time. My healing was complete.

From far overhead came the shrill caw of a crow, ear splitting and startling. We jumped apart as if caught committing a crime.

John shook a fist up over his head in mock anger. "Darn bird! Things were just getting interesting!" His gaze dropped to me, but before our eyes met, I looked away.

John didn't push. "Let's go check out that ice before it's pitch dark here. Wouldn't want to get lost on the way back home."

My eyes widened. "Could that happen?"

He smiled. "No."

I believed him.

CHAPTER TEN

Needless to say, there was a slight shift in our relationship after that walk in the woods. Mary didn't need to be told that something was different. As John and I pulled off boots and coats, she simply looked from him to me and winked. I could feel my cheeks coloring and turned away, fussing with my hat and mittens.

Each day as we worked, we became more informal, less stilted. Oh, he still made me work just as hard — it had only been one kiss, after all — but he had altered his tone.

It took me the better part of a week to enter the data he'd so easily dismissed as "preliminary," and by then he had accumulated even more.

"So, how are you planning to tackle this?" I asked one morning as we were getting underway.

He beetled his brows, shifting a bulging file folder from one arm to the other. "What do you mean?"

"Well, I mean, how will you be dividing up your work — historical versus crime-solving? How much time on the history part? How much time examining the murder?"

John reached up to rub the side of his nose. "Hmmm. It's still early days, of course, but I've been thinking I could turn the major portion of historical research over to you. You've got enough experience to at least begin that process." He looked at me for confirmation.

I bobbed my head. "I'm sure I can handle that."

"And that will leave me free to dig further into the recent past. Ask some people some questions."

"Where were you on the night of?" I said jokingly.

His eyes grew dark and somber. "Exactly, Gretchen. That's exactly it."

"I've got to tell you, your part sounds a lot more interesting. Like a made-for-TV movie."

John smiled. "I'll be off chasing suspects while you're here doing the equivalent of watching home movies."

I wrinkled my nose. It sounded even less appealing when phrased that way.

He chucked me under the chin. "Who knows, Gretchen? Maybe the key to all this lies in the past, and you'll be the one to find it."

"Oh, I don't know about that." I moved to the computer desk. "I thought the murdered man was your grandfather's business partner. That would certainly seem to indicate the trouble is of recent vintage."

"Yes." John's answer was brief.

I wondered if he'd rather not discuss the murder, then decided it didn't matter. Eventually, he'd have to share all his information with me if he expected me to type it!

"What are your thoughts on this, John? Who do you think is guilty?" I couldn't help recalling Al's conversation with Mary. Al thought he knew who was responsible. Did he? How?

John sat on the edge of his desk, one leg swinging. "My best guess is that it had to be someone else connected to that business. An employee? Another partner? But how many partners were there? I don't know!" He answered his own question, his fist smacking the desktop in frustration. "No one — no one — has been able to find any papers related to this particular deal. It's like it never happened. Never existed!"

"What was the deal, anyhow? Something financial, wasn't it?" Wasn't it always?

"Yes. A real estate deal. Hundreds of acres of farmland to be developed into an upscale subdivision. Despicable enough, just like that. But then it turned out all the land was on a flood plain. The houses already under construction were seriously damaged, and of course, all the buyers wanted their money back. And the money had been . . ." he paused, lifted his hands, ". . . supposedly, reinvested."

"So, your family was facing financial ruin," I put in.

John hesitated before responding. "I don't know if it would have ruined Gramps, but the scandal alone was enough to nearly kill him. He's a very proud man."

"And the dead man? The partner?"

"From what I understand, and mind you I certainly don't have all the answers. That's what I hope to do here. From what I understand Jim Gallagher had the idea for the deal, but no capital. Gramps let him be in charge, just supplied the cash."

I bit my lip. "Rather naïve of him, hmm?"

John came quickly to the old man's defense. "I don't know. I'm sure there were plenty of deals in the past where the Honeycutts were silent partners. This just shouldn't have been one of them."

"And then, because of, what? The scandal? Your grandfather allegedly killed Gallagher?" The story unfolded piece by dramatic piece.

"Thereby creating an even bigger scandal! See, Gretchen, that simply isn't logical!" John jumped from the desktop and began to circle the room in big, ranging strides. "If he wanted to avoid scandal, the very last thing he'd do is commit a crime. And he isn't even physically able to commit such a crime!"

The fervor of his belief in his grandfather was stirring, almost overwhelming, but it was too soon for me to declare the man innocent after the scales of justice had deemed him guilty. I steered the conversation back to the mystery man, Jim Gallagher.

"This Gallagher, where did he come from? How did your grandfather become involved with him?"

"I don't know! No one seems to know! You know, all of us grandkids have our own lives. Most of us don't live around here anymore, don't have that much contact on a day-to-day basis with Gramps. Certainly, we're not privy to details of every business transaction of Honeycutt, Inc."

"No, of course not," I placated. "But the

generation before yours? Your parents? His children?"

John sighed, pushing one hand through his thick, dark hair. My eyes followed the motion, and I swallowed hard, feeling the pull of attraction. I wanted to run my own fingers through that hair, give it a tug while he kissed me . . . Clearing my throat, I banished the vision. What, oh, what would dear Sandy think if she knew where her job lead had taken me?

"The Honeycutts are just as dysfunctional as every family, Gretchen. As you should know. As everyone should know!" He gestured expansively, dramatically. "Our news is always trotted out in the tabloids. There should be a law!"

I swiveled in my chair. Back and forth, back and forth. "Well, there are libel laws."

"Yes, but usually the stories they run are true!" He was exasperated, his frustration printed clearly on his face — brows knit, eyes dark, lips pressed into a firm, uncompromising line.

"Oh, dear. That would present some complications," I agreed.

"Too many complications." He broke off, massaging his temples with the tips of his fingers. "I don't want to talk about this anymore. That's been the problem all along.

Too much talk, not enough action."

Feeling duly chastened, I swiveled swiftly back to face the computer screen. "Sorry," I muttered.

"Oh, hey, I didn't mean you," John's exclamation came quickly. "It's okay for you to ask questions. I expect us to do a lot more talking as we sort this thing out. I mean me! I've spent too long thinking about doing something, saying I'm going to do something. Promising Gramps. Now that I'm here, now that I've hired you, I've got to make it happen."

"When did you see your grandfather last? How's he doing?"

The prison, I knew, wasn't far from there. It was located in a small town about an hour's ride south. I had seen it only once, from the highway, on a trip with my parents. It had made quite an impression on me at the tender age of ten or eleven, when issues of right and wrong were still blissfully separate. No gray areas. No injustice. Those were the days. The compound had loomed, dark and forbidding even on a summer day. There were lookout towers at each corner and, although I didn't see any armed guards, I knew they were there. Barbed wire — the first I'd ever seen — crawled along the top of the fence, menacing and threatening bodily harm.

John must have been recalling a similar, sinister vision because in response to my question, he grimaced in pain. "I saw him two weeks ago. He looked . . . old. He looked tired." He moved to the window, his back to me, and I knew he was struggling with emotion. "He's gotten so frail," John went on without turning around. "As if he's given up hope. I have to get him out of there soon, or I'm afraid it will be too late."

Across the room, a clock ticked over the mantel, a potent reminder of time passing.

"Would you like to meet him? You could come along for my conference appointment."

"Conference appointment?"

"Yes," John said. "I've arranged with the warden to meet with Gramps privately to discuss the case."

"Huh. I didn't know you could do that. I thought, you know," I sketched a wall in the air with my hands, "that glass panel and telephones. Like on TV."

Nodding, John explained. "Yes, that's the way our visits usually are. This time, though, I'd like a bit of privacy."

I smiled. "Looks like the Honeycutt name can still open doors. Literally."

The minute the words left my mouth, I wanted to call them back. John's eyes darkened, and a crease of anger appeared at the corner of his mouth.

"Gretchen." He spoke my name like my third grade teacher. "This is not a special favor because my family is powerful. This is S.O.P. Standard operating procedure. With sufficient just cause, the director of the facility can grant permission for private visits. From attorneys. From relatives. From other officials." He ticked them off on his fingers. "Got it?"

"Got it," I repeated, chastened. Of course a man like John wouldn't use his family position for personal gain or preferential treatment. "Sorry."

He sighed. "S'okay. It's just that . . . I get that a lot, you know. That implication. And it makes me angry."

John thought a moment in silence, tapping one finger against his jawbone. When he spoke, there was no trace of anger in his tone. "I'm going tomorrow. Leaving early. We could make a day of it." He was excited, the words coming fast, peppered.

"Sort of like a field trip," I suggested.

"That's right. We can make a few other stops along the way. See a few people . . ."

"In relation to the book?"

"Of course."

Of course.

CHAPTER ELEVEN

I didn't sleep well that night before our trip. We'd had chocolate cake for dessert at dinner, and I'd eaten way too much of it. The caffeine set my nerves a jangle and even a long soak in a hot tub didn't calm me down.

Sitting up in bed, I tried to read for a while, but my concentration just wasn't there. I read words but didn't take them in. Eventually, I gave up, tossing the paperback onto the floor beside me and reaching for my sketchbook.

I knew my subject matter before I began, so the pencil moved swiftly in my hand. Ten minutes later, John's face looked back at me. I'd drawn him in a serious mood, the way I saw him so frequently at his desk. That finger rested against his jaw, as usual, and a tiny crease marked the space between his eyebrows. It had taken longer to capture the quirk of his lips. I'd licked my own as I drew them, recalling our first kiss at the pond and the few other kisses we'd stolen since then. The memory made me smile, made me add an extra bit of sparkle to John's eyes when I sketched them.

Holding the finished product at arm's length, I nodded, pleased with myself. Maybe someday I'd show it to him. Maybe I'd keep it a secret, just for me.

As I added my initials and the date to the bottom corner, a shiver ran down my back. I shrugged it away without thinking. Only when it came again, just a breath of air on the back of my neck, did I stiffen. Spinning around, I saw what I knew I'd see. Nothing at all.

It wasn't snowing tonight. The wind wasn't blowing huge gusts of icy Canadian air against the windows. In fact, the bedroom was warm as toast. Until now. Until that blasted draft.

Bringing my hand up, I rubbed the nape of my neck, the very spot where I'd felt the touch of the air — and felt it yet again, this time accompanied by the very faintest of odors. I twitched my nose and blinked, doubting the evidence of my senses.

It took me a moment to identify the scent. I sniffed again, long and hard, concentrating.

"Violets!" I exclaimed, amazed. "It's violets!"

There were no flowers in my room, I knew. The little bouquet which had been fresh in a vase the week before was long since gone. An artificial arrangement sat on top of the dresser across the room, beautiful, but definitely unscented.

There could be only one explanation, of course. An old house, cold spots, the aroma of flowers when none were present.

This room was haunted. I was sleeping in a room with a ghost!

The idea seemed so ludicrous, I had to laugh, but the sound was jagged and uneven, a nervous laugh.

"If we're going to be sharing a room," I said, pacing the open space around the bed. "It would be nice to know your name. Mine is Gretchen."

I waited, standing in front of the big mirror over the dresser. I didn't look haunted, I decided as I checked out my reflection. This country air agreed with me. My cheeks were fuller and not so pale. That could be due to Mary's good cooking, as could the slight thickening of my waistline. I grimaced. No more dessert!

Blinking, I focused again on the old mirror, cloudy with age. I didn't expect to see

91

any shadows behind me, any face looking back, and there were none.

"Ghosts don't show up in mirrors, anyway," I told myself, needing to hear the normalcy of my own voice. "No, it's vampires who don't reflect." I was babbling, prattling on. My heart was beating in a noticeable way, and I realized my palms were damp when I clasped my hands together.

I sighed. "Look, whoever you are, I really have to get some sleep. I won't bug you if you don't bug me, okay?" I raised my eyebrows and turned in a slow circle, surveying my room.

All was peaceful. The violet smell had faded. I felt — I was — truly alone.

With some trepidation, I climbed into bed and shut off the lights. The covers tucked up under my chin, I lay motionless, listening to my own breathing. How could I possibly sleep when I kept expecting chains to clank and moans to begin? A mighty yawn overtook me. How was I ever going to get a moment's rest? I forced my eyes closed. How would I. . . .

When I woke, the sun was shining and someone was pounding on the bedroom door.

"Rise and shine, Gretchen! It's after eight o'clock!" John sounded eager and cheery, two annoying traits to display so early in the morning.

"Be right down!" I called, kicking at the covers. I have never been accused of being an early bird, but I tried to put a good face on it, hurrying through shower and makeup. Standing in front of the mirror, I yanked a brush swiftly through my hair, then closed my eyes to French braid it. It took longer to decide what to wear. I wanted to make a good impression.

At last, I settled on my best sweater — a soft pink cardigan detailed with embroidery — pairing it with a full black skirt that hung to my ankles. The effect was feminine but not frilly. Not too casual, not too tailored.

"Just right!" I quoted Goldilocks, adding earrings and just a touch of perfume.

From downstairs, the chime of a grandfather clock drifted up. By the time it had finished counting the hours, I was slipping into my seat at the breakfast table.

John looked up from his bowl of oatmeal, nodding approval at either my attire or my arrival. He was a quiet man over breakfast, I'd learned, preferring to bury himself in the morning newspaper. I'd begun bringing a book down with me, so I could read, too.

Immediately after the meal he pushed back his chair and said, "Gretchen, I'll meet you at the front door in five minutes. Al's bringing the car around for us."

Ten minutes later, we stood side by side on the front porch. I stamped my feet to keep warm and looked off in the direction of the garage.

"Any sign of him?"

"None," John sighed. "We could have walked there in the time we've wasted waiting. Let's go!" He led the way down the steps and across the circle drive, swinging his briefcase with each step. "It's not like Al to forget things," he said. "I'm a bit surprised."

We headed down a brief service drive lined with evergreens. At the end of the lane, a bulky brick stable was visible. The horses had long since gone and the building now served as a garage.

There were four wooden doors, all of them closed except the one where John's car was housed. When we entered our boots made thumping, echoing sounds on the concrete. Puddles of water marked the floor where clods of snow had fallen from the car's underside and melted. A faint odor of motor oil and gasoline filled the air.

There was no sign of Al.

"Al!" John barked the man's name.

In the silence that followed, the only sound was the gentle, rhythmic drip of more melting snow.

"You go that way," I pointed to the right. "And I'll go this way, and the first one to find him wins a prize."

We headed off on our search, meeting up at the office located at the back of the building. It, too, was deserted, but signs of life were evident. A knit cap was tossed on the desktop, a cup of coffee was growing cold beside it.

John surveyed the scene, his expression having shifted from merely irritated to downright angry. "If he's at least left the keys behind, we can hit the road." He turned to a pegboard sheet filled with keys, marked and unmarked.

"Wait a minute!" I held up one hand.

Far off, the clang of footsteps could be heard, moving swiftly in our direction. John crossed both arms over his chest, leaning back against the wall. When Al appeared in the doorway, cheeks flushed and out of breath, John spoke. "Where in the blue blazes have you been, Al? We've been waiting half an hour!"

Al stopped dead, startled, it seemed, by our unexpected appearance. His eyes were narrowed, by irritation or anger. Hands on his hips, he didn't reply to John's remark, just shook his head and moved to the pegboard. When he turned around to face us with the key in his hand, the anger was less visible. I could still sense it bubbling just under his now apologetic exterior.

"Hey, I'm really sorry, John. I just lost track of time. Got busy with a project. Those windows, you know?"

John cut him off. "Whatever. Just give me the keys." He stretched out one hand, palm up. After Al relinquished the key, John gave a very brief smile. "We'll be back by dinner."

Once we were in the car, traveling slowly down the long driveway, I said casually, "Al seemed angry. You don't suppose he and Mary had a fight?"

John's answer was a snort. "Gretchen, if those two had had a fight, we'd all know about it. Their blowups are rare, but quite vocal. We'd have heard them half a mile away."

This idea was startling. They certainly didn't seem like knockdown, drag-out brawlers. I'd have guessed Al blustered and Mary blustered back until one or the other quickly subsided into a days-long silence.

"Well, he was mad about something." I

settled back in my seat, adjusting the belt across my lap.

Stopping the car and carefully checking for traffic before pulling out, John seemed thoughtful. "Yes," he said at last. "I'll have to speak to him. He still hasn't reported on his visit to the cottage, either. I'm assuming that means everything was fine, and there's nothing to report."

I hadn't forgotten about the footprints, or about that sense of someone watching me in the woods that day. Just the memory made my skin creep. Looking out the window, I watched the fields and woods roll by, remembering that other odd occurrence at Mill Hollow.

"You know, Mill Hollow is a creepy kind of place," I stated. I pushed my cold feet closer to the heat vent on the floor. "In fact, I think it's haunted. My room is haunted."

If I expected John to laugh at such nonsense or be shocked by my statements, I was doomed to disappointment. Without taking his eyes from the road, he said simply, "Tell me about it."

So I did, recounting the cold draft and my search for its source. When I got to the part about the violets, he cut me off.

"Violets! You got to smell them?" He

darted a glance at me, looking surprised and excited.

"Y-yes." I frowned. "Have you smelled them, too?"

"Oh, no, no. Wish I had, though. It's a family legend. One of the great aunts lived out her life in that room. Never married. Never wanted to, I guess. Anyway, it was kind of tragic. Or it seems so now. A wasted life . . ."

"Maybe she was happy single. Not everyone needs to be married, you know." I sprang to the maiden aunt's defense.

John signaled to pull onto the freeway. As we accelerated, he laughed. "And a lot of married people would be better off alone." He shook his head. "Hope I never make that mistake."

"What? Getting married?"

"No." He looked over, into my eyes. "Marrying the wrong person."

His sentence hung in the air, weighted with emphasis. Our budding relationship was just that — barely underway. I bit my lip and blinked. Was it too early to share history? I cleared my throat. No, it wasn't.

"My parents were divorced. It was awful."

And it had been. The fragmented childhood had come after years of sitting in the dark, listening to arguing from the other room.

John's hand slipped off the wheel and reached across to squeeze mine. I looked up, gave a weak smile and a shrug.

"I'm grown up, now. The past doesn't matter." Brave words.

"The past always matters, Gretchen."

"What about you? Happy childhood in the bosom of your extended family?" I made the words faintly sarcastic without meaning to. Jealousy, I suppose.

John tipped his head to one side. "Pretty much so. During the summer and on holidays, it was great. But we were all sent off to boarding schools, you know. That wasn't so hot." He scowled. "Wasn't as bad once we were older — high school, maybe. Before that, it was tough to be away from home."

"From your Mom and Dad," I put in, nodding. I could understand missing parents, all right.

John drove on in silence and I could see he was turning the idea over in his mind. His lips quirked, and he blinked once or twice. "I've got to tell you, no. That wasn't what I missed." He gave a hollow laugh. "Don't I sound heartless? I missed my stuff — my toys, my bike. I missed my dog. But my parents? No, didn't miss them. Of course, we kids didn't get to know them very well."

"Were they of the be-seen-and-not-heard variety?"

"Yes, definitely. We did have a nice nanny, though."

As if that were consolation enough.

"So your privileged childhood wasn't so privileged."

"Nothing is ever as it seems, Gretchen."

"You don't have to tell me that!" I exclaimed, then quickly veered off the subject. "Do you mind if we play the radio?" I was already reaching for the knob, turning on the all-talk station. I was feeling momentarily all talked out.

CHAPTER TWELVE

"Gramps!"

John loped forward to envelop the frail old man in a big bear hug. His grandfather clapped him on the back. His hands, I noticed, were thin and covered with bulgy blue veins.

I stayed back, letting the reunion take place. We were in a nondescript conference room located close to the office area of the prison facility. One lone guard stood at the door, making his presence known without uttering a sound. I was feeling a little uneasy. Claustrophobic, even though the room was big enough. Just the idea of the bars on the windows made it difficult for me to take a deep breath. Was this how animals felt in the zoo — locked in forever?

"Gramps, I'd like you to meet my new research assistant, Gretchen Waller. She's going to help me with the book. And with finding the real killer." John waved me forward.

Smiling broadly, I extended a hand. "It's a pleasure to meet you, Mr. Honeycutt."

Henry Hanover Honeycutt, American legend and millionaire, was above average height — or had been in his prime. He was just over six feet tall and prison life had made him lean, stringy. Salt-and-pepper, but mostly salty, hair stood up around his head, in need of an appointment with a hairbrush. Deep creases ran vertically down his cheeks, making already prominent cheekbones leap into sharp relief. John had his eyes, I realized, and his smile.

Henry clasped my hand firmly in his, then gave me a quick once over. "It's been a long time since I've seen a pretty gal," he said. "Gretchen, you're a sight for these tired, old eyes."

"Gramps, you'll never change," John chided gently.

"That's the only good thing about getting old, John." He gave me a watery wink. "You can say anything you want, and nobody will tell you otherwise."

John motioned the older man over toward the rectangular table that stood in the middle of the room. He took a seat opposite his grandfather, and I took my place next to my boss. I made sure I was sitting so I could see the door. Just in case.

"It's good to see you still have your sense of humor, Gramps," John said, pulling in his chair.

I took out my notebook, uncapped my pen, ready to get down to business.

His grandfather lifted denim-clad shoulders. "No sense in losing it. You need one around here." Darting his eyes around the room, he indicated the whole facility in one gesture.

John's eyes clouded, and his brows knit together. His concern for his aging grandfather was clear on his face. Inching forward, he leaned across the table, asking earnestly, "How are you, Gramps? Really?"

Henry rapped out a rhythm on the tabletop, looking first one way and then the other before responding. "Really? I'm okay." He sounded surprised and looked it, eyes wide, lips drawn in a smile. Nodding to confirm the words, he went on, "I'm doing all right. Of course, I'd be lying if I didn't say I'd rather be out of here and back at Mill Hollow. But," he shrugged, "I've made a few very interesting friends." His eyebrows darted up and down to indicate just how interesting.

"I can imagine!" I said, as John clucked

his tongue like a mother hen.

After another ten minutes or so of general conversation, we got down to the matter at hand. John recapped the work he had done on the biography, making me detail my work with the historical bits, then sketched out what he hoped to do, crime-wise.

"I'm going to do my own investigation, Gramps. Talk to anyone you suggest. There has to be enough evidence to have you released. The police never even looked." His fist landed hard on the tabletop, a gesture I was getting very used to. "It was just easier to arrest you and forget about something as inconsequential as justice!"

"Oh, now, John, calm down. The guard will think we're starting our own riot." He chuckled. "You young people are so excitable, and I'll tell you, blowing steam won't get you anywhere with this."

I could forgive him for sounding cynical.

"You have an alibi for the time of the murder, right?" I asked.

Henry sighed heavily. "Yes, I do. But they just used it against me. I was out walking Big Nick that night. It was late, but it was summer and just barely dark. He's a big dog, likes to walk a long way, so we did. We were even quite close to where the body was found. I've always wondered how differently things would have gone if I'd been the one to find him . . ." He trailed off, shaking his head in slow bemusement at the circumstances.

"Who did? Find him, I mean?" The details were new to me. I opened the notebook I'd brought along and licked the tip of my pencil.

"Al did." John supplied the answer. "The morning after the murder. Assumed it was a poacher or a vagrant, met with foul play. Until the man was recognized."

"Your business partner." I looked to Henry.

He scoffed. "Some partner. I gave him thousands and he lost it all. The man was nothing but a criminal. A con man." One long finger stabbed in John's direction. "Your father tried to warn me, but I wouldn't listen. First time Martin's ever been right about anything."

Beside me I could sense John tensing, straightening up. His hands tightened on the edge of the table, but he remained silent.

"But how did they turn walking the dog into evidence against you?" I twirled my pencil between my palms.

"Well, my own testimony put me at the scene, dear. Or near enough. I didn't have any humans along to verify my words, and

Big Nick isn't talking." He grinned at the feeble joke.

John pressed his lips together until they formed one solid, forbidding line. "If only someone else had seen you! Leaving the house or even returning. They could prove you were telling the truth."

"Not really." I was the devil's advocate. "You'd need a witness to your time in the woods. Your path. Otherwise," it was my turn to shrug, "they would just say you were out of the house at the right time, for the right length of time."

"Exactly! That's just what happened!" Henry crowed. "But, you see, there is something important no one pursued. That rotten attorney of mine was so sure I wouldn't need to defend myself. He wouldn't let me take the stand! Then I could have told the truth!" His voice rose, prompting the guard at the door to turn and examine the scene with a frown.

"Gramps, what are you talking about?" John's question was barely a whisper. "What are you saying?"

The old man blinked, his eyes swimming, more from excitement than sadness. When he spoke, his voice was raspy, the words coming ever so slowly so we'd be sure to understand.

"I wasn't alone that night in the woods. Somebody else was there!"

CHAPTER THIRTEEN

"What?" The word exploded from John's mouth. He pushed back his chair and rose automatically, hands braced on the table.

Beside him I sat frozen, looking from boss to convict.

"Who was it? Why didn't you tell me this sooner? Did you recognize them?" The questions came rapid fire.

Henry smiled complacently at the guard who was once more standing at attention, eyes narrowed in our direction. "It's okay, Ralph. Nothing to worry about." Still smiling, he looked up to John and whispered, "Land's sake, sit down, you fool! You're determined to get me in trouble today."

Chastised, John dropped inch by inch back into his seat. "Actually, I'm trying to get you out! Now, tell me this story!"

"Big Nick and I were deep in the woods, not too far from the cottage. Maybe five hundred feet from where the body was.

Anyway, I thought I heard something. Not the usual sounds of the forest. Something more definite, somehow." He closed his eyes, opened and closed both hands as he searched for the right words. "There was the sound of movement. Just a sort of swish, and then — nothing. Silence, but a silence like someone holding his breath. Do you know what I mean?" Henry looked to me with hopeful eyes.

Did I know? Too well. He was describing my own experience in those woods. I swallowed over the lump in my throat. "Sure do!"

"All right, then." He returned to the scene. "So, I called out. 'Hello? Anybody there?' But, of course, no one answered. Big Nick headed off in that direction, his fur all on end."

I shuddered at the image. A dark and lonely wood. One old man, one old dog. Defenseless.

"You should have turned around and run for home!" I rubbed my hands up and down my arms.

"Couldn't leave Big Nick!" Henry was shocked at my suggestion. "As it was, he didn't go too far. Good dog, Nick. Stopped in his tracks and didn't move 'til I got there and snapped the lead on his collar. I had to hold him tight then though. He started growling and pulling. It was obvious someone was nearby. Whoever it was heard the dog, and it spooked 'em. There was a crashing in the underbrush. Someone rushing around, away. I saw a shape. Could have been a man or a woman. At that distance, it was impossible to tell. Especially since my eyes aren't as young as they once were."

"Did you notice anything at all that could identify this person? The way they ran, what they wore? Anything?" John was desperate for a way to follow this lead. He spread his hands, repeating, "Anything?"

Henry rubbed one hand over his chin, as if that would help him remember. "Didn't have a limp or anything obvious like that, John. All I saw was a figure in a dark coat running for all get out."

"What color was the coat?" I asked.

"Darkish, I think. Black. Or blue. Can't be sure."

John and I waited in silence while Henry closed his eyes to conjure up the scene.

"Might have been maroon. And the buttons were gold. I remember that, catching just a flash of them." He concentrated further, grimacing with the very effort, then shook his head in frustration. "Nope, that's it. That's all I can say for sure. Not much to go on, is it?"

John's shrug was eloquent. "It's a place to start, I guess. We'll visit the neighbors on the way home. I'm sure it wasn't one of them — they'd have no reason to run when you called."

I had a question rolling around in my brain and now seemed a good time to ask it. "Since it was summer, was Mill Hollow full of visitors? Who else was on the estate at the time?" Perhaps John already had this information, but I didn't.

"Let me think. We'd had a full house the week before, but nearly everyone had gone on home." He looked to John. "Just your aunt and uncle were there."

John nodded. "Yes, I know Bert and Doris." His nostrils widened as if he smelled something unpleasant.

"Yep. They always did overstay their welcome." Henry was frank. "It doesn't help that they live so close."

"They have a house about forty miles from Mill Hollow," John explained to me. "They were frequent visitors, the way I understand it."

"Were?" Why the past tense, I wondered.

Henry snorted. "Since all this happened, they haven't been shining around. I don't flatter myself that it's because I'm not there any more. If they missed me, they'd come visit here. But they never have."

I could detect a note of disappointment beneath his bitterness. A familiar story, alone and abandoned. But not by John.

"Ah, you're better off without them." John waved his hands, as if he could physically dispel the image of the couple. "I suppose I'll have to grit my teeth and stop to see them."

"Better than having a tooth pulled," Henry joked.

John groaned. "Just barely."

"You're lucky, John. Doris always seemed rather fond of you."

"Is that a blessing or a curse?"

The two went on in this vein a few minutes longer, lamenting and cajoling. It all made me very eager to meet this set of Honeycutts. Later, in the car on the way to their property I asked about Bert and Doris.

John scowled. "Well, you know every family has to have the relatives no one can stand. The greedy moochers. The ones always making tactless remarks." He waited for me to nod as faces sprang to mind. "We have Bert and Doris." He gave a shudder. "Brrr!"

"It's as bad as all that?"

112

"You'll see," he promised.
I did.

CHAPTER FOURTEEN

No one was home at Bert and Doris's. A housekeeper informed us they had gone off for the weekend. The relief on John's face was quite evident when he expressed disappointment at missing them.

"Can't say I'm not glad," he told me as we headed back to Mill Hollow after stopping for a quick lunch. "But now I'm delayed again."

"It must be so frustrating for you," I said, adding in a droll tone. "Of course, I still have buckets of typing to do."

John glanced over, smiling widely. "And I have a secret." His eyes glinted, looking more golden than green.

"Oh?"

With one hand on the wheel, he fished in the pocket of his jacket, then triumphantly held up a scrap of paper covered in numbers.

"Gramps slipped me this when I was saying goodbye. 'Look in the safe,' he said. So, I will!"

He pressed down on the accelerator and we hurried home.

When I opened the front door at Mill Hollow my nose wrinkled instinctively. What was that smell? Pungent, woody, it defied identification at first. Beside me, John sniffed the air, as well. We reached a conclusion simultaneously.

"It's a pipe!" I said, turning to him for confirmation.

"It's Uncle Bert," John said with little enthusiasm.

"No kidding!"

John pointed wordlessly at the coat rack. An unfamiliar plaid Mac hung off one peg, a lady's checked wool beside it.

"And Aunt Doris." The addition was unnecessary.

I peeled off my gloves and stepped out of my boots. "Talk about coincidence! What a stroke of luck for you!"

"Guess the safe will have to wait 'til later, now. That figures." John's expression spoke volumes as he reached down to pat Big Nick, who had come to welcome us. At the sound of approaching footsteps, he wiped his grimace carefully away. The face John turned to the new arrival was utterly blank.

"John! John! Great to see you!" A hearty voice bellowed down the hallway. "Heard you were taking up residence, thought we'd come visit. Hope you don't mind."

The man hurrying toward us was big and bulky. Probably on the far side of sixty, he was just under six feet tall and embodied the word pudgy. He had a rolling gait, for obvious reasons, and his full, rounded cheeks were red from the exertion of crossing the long hall. Dressed as a country gentleman, he sported faded corduroys and a patterned sweater. He made no attempt to hide his curiosity about me, openly looking over and smiling even as he took John's hand.

"And who have we here, hmm?" Uncle Bert gave John a wink.

John sighed heavily, then introduced me. "She's my research assistant on the new book."

"Research, eh?" Uncle Bert shook my hand, holding it a little too long. His palm was clammy.

I forced a pleasant smile. "Pleased to meet you, Mr. Honeycutt. I've heard so much about you." And none of it good, I added mentally.

Another darted glance at John. "I'll bet

you have, my dear. Wouldn't doubt it. Doris is in the parlor, warming up by the fire. Mary's supposed to be bringing us tea . . ." His tone implied she was late with her duty. "Come join us!"

John stalled. "We'll be along in a few minutes, Uncle Bert. We need to file some paperwork first."

I flapped my notebook in confirmation.

Uncle Bert's eyes narrowed. "Where have you been? Researching?" He put a rather ugly emphasis on the word.

"If you must know, we've just returned from visiting Gramps. You may remember him?" John was bitterly sarcastic, lifting one eyebrow. "And then, in fact, after talking with him, we went looking for you."

I didn't imagine Bert stepping away. "Oh?" His grin belied his anxious expression. "Well, we'll talk in a few minutes, then." Another step back, two. He spun rather quickly on one heel and headed off the way he had come. Over one shoulder, he added, "Don't be too long, now."

I looked at John. Really, the situation was almost comical. Pressing my lips together, I puffed out my cheeks.

Laughing, John slipped his arm around my waist as we started for the library. "Just wait until you meet Aunt Doris!"

"Is that a threat?"

He evaded. "You'll see."

Aunt Doris lived up to her reputation. When John and I entered the parlor a short time later, the middle-aged woman was enthroned in the room's best chair, the tea cart conveniently located at her side. Big Nick entered the room at our heels, looked at the unexpected guests, and then turned back to the door. He settled uncomfortably onto the rug, as if ready to make a hasty retreat.

Doris beamed a greeting at us, revealing broad ivory teeth framed by purplish red lips. Actually, she was a bit heavy-handed with all her makeup, I realized as I drew closer. A mask of foundation covered her skin, heavy black eyeliner ringed close-set eyes and two perfectly round spots of blush bloomed on each full cheek. Her black hair was so black, it looked almost blue. She wore it swept back into a chignon. A long gold chain draped around her neck and attached to eyeglasses. She looked for all the world like a dowager. Minor royalty without a throne.

"Such a pleasure to meet you," she gushed as John introduced me. When she shook my hand I could feel the heavy weight of her rings pressing into my skin.

"I've been looking forward to it," I said in all honesty. Well, John had piqued my curiosity, making me eager to make her acquaintance.

Doris pressed those lips together and turned up the edges. "So sweet," she said softly and without sarcasm. "Some tea, John?"

John was ranging nervously around the room, his hands stuffed in his pockets. He didn't answer her question.

"I was telling Uncle Bert we went to see Gramps today. He told us some interesting things about the time of the murder." He paused.

If he was hoping for some sort of reaction from his aunt, he must have been disappointed. With a steady hand, she concentrated on pouring a single cup of tea. Passing it to me, she asked, "Sugar?"

I shook my head and sipped, my eyes moving rapidly from her to John.

He took a step closer, standing behind Uncle Bert's chair. "Gramps made me eager to talk to you two. He said you were staying here that weekend."

"Were we? Bert, were we?" Doris knit her eyebrows and thought.

Bert merely shifted in his chair, as if there

were tacks on the seat.

"Yes, you were." John was emphatic. "So, we need to talk about everything you might recall about that time."

"Oh, John!" Doris sat back, crossing her ankles. She wore an angora twin set and tweed skirt. Typical English country fashion. But this wasn't England. "That was two years ago! You can hardly expect a couple of old fogies like us to recall that!" She laughed off the suggestion.

I could see John's hand tighten on the back of Bert's chair, but his voice was not unpleasant when he said, "Not only do I expect it, I demand it."

"Well! I —"

"So, put on your thinking caps and do your best to refresh your memories. After dinner, we'll all get together in the library where Gretchen will record our interview."

Dark eyes growing darker still, Doris lapsed into silence, drinking from her cup and watching John over the rim.

"That's fine, Johnny boy. We'll be there," Bert blustered. "Don't think we'll be able to help much, but we'll be happy to do our part. No need to get up a head of steam over it. You know we all have your grand-dad's best interests at heart."

"I'm sure you do," John was unconvincing. "We'll see you at dinner. Gretchen?"

In silence, I followed my employer from the room. When the door was safely closed behind us he let out a monumental sigh.

"You certainly let them have it," I said. "Was that wise?"

His green eyes darted over at me, flashing with a second of doubt, not anger. Then, he nodded. "Yes, I think so. You don't know them like I do. If I don't press, they'll merely hem and haw."

"But what if they don't know anything? Wouldn't they have come forward if they did?"

John arched his eyebrows. "I'd like to think so, but I can't be sure. So instead I'll play the heavy."

"You know, it's an old phrase, but you catch more flies with honey . . ."

John grinned. He slipped an arm around my shoulders and drew me closer as we walked back in the direction of the library. "Well, that sounds like a good job assignment for you. Befriend Aunt Doris."

"Hmm." I pondered the tall order.

"I'll make it worth your while," he teased.

"Oh?" This could be interesting.

"I'll let you turn the lock on the safe." His eyes were wide at the exciting idea.

Before I could respond, we heard rapid

footsteps coming from behind.

"John!" It was Mary, her cheeks ruddy, her hands clenched. She hurried toward us, all but running. "John, I hope it's all right about Bert and Doris. They just showed up here, sweet as you please, just like in the old days. Well," she glanced from John to me, looking almost helpless. "I didn't know what to do, so I let them in and gave them tea and prayed you'd show up soon. You know, they have a lot of nerve —"

John cut off what could have easily become a tirade, taking both Mary's hands and saying, "It's okay, Mary. You did the only gracious thing you could do. Yes, they're a trial, but, as it turns out, we were hoping to see them."

My ears pricked up at the "we." That was us! John and me! The idea made me feel warm deep inside, like I'd just been hugged.

Mary frowned, stunned by the idea anyone would choose to seek out Bert and Doris. "Really?"

"Yep." John quickly related his grand-father's story about hearing someone else in the woods.

It was an intriguing tale. Mary's eyes never left John's face as he told it.

"Well! Well!" She seemed at a loss for words.

"Isn't it wonderful?" I put in. "A genuine lead to follow. John will be able to prove Gramps' innocence, I just know it!" I made my own response more enthusiastic than justified, because Mary's reaction seemed so odd, too quiet. If I went over the top, she'd be forced to show some sort of emotion.

The older woman shifted her weight. "Yes, that's marvelous news, John. Someone else in the woods. Probably the murderer. I wonder who?" Her voice trailed off and her gaze drifted away. Then, after a moment's thought, she focused in on John's first remark. "What does that have to do with Bert and Doris?"

Spreading his hands, John gave the simple explanation. "They were here at the time of the murder. They could have seen something, heard something —"

Mary chuckled, leaning back. "Those two? Remember something?" She gave John a playful slap on the arm. "Oh, that's rich. I hope you haven't hung all your plans on those two!" Her white hair bobbed as she shook her head.

"It's the only thing I've found so far, so I'm going to thoroughly check it out."

"He's going to interrogate them after dinner," I said.

"Interview," John corrected with subtlety.

I shrugged. "Same thing."

"Well, good luck to you," Mary offered. "You know, I think you'd have a better chance of proving those two did it than of getting a straight answer out of either one."

Obviously, the idea of Bert and/or Doris as a murderer was an entertaining one, because she laughed again. Just before turning away, she said, "Dinner's at six tonight, by the by."

We headed back toward the library.

"She certainly didn't give the news a rousing endorsement," John said, his voice heavy.

"No, she didn't." There was something about her reaction that bothered me, niggling at the back of my mind. I wasn't sure how to put it in words, but gave it a try, anyway. "John, didn't it seem odd how Mary looked when you told her about the possibility of someone else in the woods?"

He frowned. "She seemed sort of quiet."

We were at the library door now. After opening it, he waved me through.

"And," I continued, "I don't know, almost anxious somehow."

"Really?" John asked. "I guess I didn't notice."

He shut the door behind us, and I wandered to my workstation, still worrying the detail.

Leaning one elbow on the desktop, I went on. "It was almost as if she knew what you were going to say."

"But how would Mary know Gramps thought someone else was in the woods that night?"

"How indeed?" I quirked a brow.

I had information John didn't. I had the tidbit of conversation overheard outside the kitchen. Ever since, I'd held it back, not knowing how John would respond to eavesdropping, especially when it might lead to questions about old family friends.

Crossing my arms over my chest, I paced across the carpet between my desk and John's. "You know, I've got to tell you . . . ," I began uncertainly.

John swiveled around to look at me, openly curious. "Tell me what?"

"Well, it's probably nothing," I qualified before relating the conversation between Mary and Al. When I'd finished, I shrugged. "I don't know. To me, it sounded like Al thought he might know who was responsible. Like he and Mary wouldn't want that information to come out."

John didn't say anything. One hand came up, and he rubbed at his jaw.

Letting him ponder, I watched in silence for a moment or two. Oh, he was a good-looking man! Not model handsome, perhaps, but definitely an eye-catcher. I let my eyes linger on the curl of his hair, then had to resist the urge to scoot across the room and give it a tug. He'd filled out a little, I noticed as I continued my inspection. While Mary's good cooking was detrimental to my statistics, it was certainly enhancing his.

"Gretchen, it's awfully hard for me to concentrate with you staring at me like that," he complained in a good-natured way. "I hope you like what you see."

As if I'd tell him what I was thinking! "Oh, stop fishing for compliments! There's a mystery to be solved here!" My smile made my cheeks pinch, and I struggled to subdue it.

John just shook his head, laughing softly in his warm, buttery tone. "I'll talk to Mary, casually —" he began.

"But, don't —"

He went on over my protest. "I won't mention your name. I'll just sort of," he wobbled a hand, searching for the words, "go fishing. It's always been easier to talk with Mary."

"I'd believe that!"

Picking up a pen, John made himself a note, I supposed about this conversation. Looking up, he said, "You're proving yourself to be quite an asset with those eagle ears of yours."

"Don't you mean eagle eyes?" I laughed.

"Well, you know what I mean, I'm sure."

"I am sure," I stated. "You mean I'm nosy." Tipping up my nose, I did my best to act offended.

"No, no. Not at all." John paused, then added thoughtfully, "Although I'll certainly watch what I say when you're not in the room. You'd probably be just outside, listening at the keyhole!"

"John!" Did he honestly think I made a habit of eavesdropping?

"Oh, relax. I'm joking."

He held up a crumpled scrap of paper. "Gramps told me to look in the safe. Now, we will."

There was an air of excitement in the room as we crossed over to the wall where a watercolor landscape hung over a green moiré ribbon.

"It's just like in the movies!" I exclaimed, watching John move the picture out of the way as if it were a door. The silent hinges were impossible to see when the picture was in place.

John looked over at me and smiled. His hand stilled on the lock, he said, "That's just what I used to think when I was a kid."

Our eyes met in understanding, and the strength of it made my knees shake.

"Would you like to do the honors?" he asked, stepping back from the safe.

"Sure!" I didn't hesitate, stepping right up and delicately grasping the little numbered dial. Following the numbers written on the paper John held, I spun the dial and pulled at the handle. "I guess it's been a while since this has been used. It's gotten stiff. You try."

John did his best. I could hear the metal grinding ever so slightly. Then, with a final wrench of his wrist, the handle turned, the door popped open and a ticker tape parade took place as thousands of papers cascaded out onto the floor.

"Oh!" I jumped forward, attempting to catch the papers as they fell, holding them in, while John snatched up the computer paper box behind his desk. One swift motion dumped the computer paper onto John's chair, then John was at my side, holding the box and signaling me to let loose the deluge.

When everything that could fall out had,

we lifted out the things which remained. There was a steel box about six inches square, a fabric pouch tied shut with braided cord and several manila envelopes carefully glued shut. The computer box brimmed over when we added the papers gathered up from the floor. John carried it to a spot I hastily cleared on my desktop.

With my hands on my hips, I peered eagerly inside. "Ok, John, what are we supposed to look for?"

The eyes that met mine looked startled, almost blank. He lifted his shoulders in a shrug. "I have no idea," he told me. "Gramps didn't say!"

CHAPTER FIFTEEN

"You'll know it when you see it," John quoted, returning from a very brief telephone conversation with his grandfather.

"That's it? No clues!"

"No clues." John ran his hand through his hair, puzzling.

"You know, it seems to me he could be a little more helpful. You are trying to save him, after all." I poked a finger into the box.

John sighed. "He said, 'If I tell you what to look for, that's all you'll see. I don't want to color your opinion.' " Another sigh. "He's right, of course."

"Of course."

I made a deliberate motion of pushing up the sleeves of my sweater. "Well, let's have at it, then. Time's a wastin'!"

When John's job description had requested someone with organizational skills, I'd had no idea I'd end up sorting seemingly endless batches of paper, photographs and newspaper clippings into more seemingly endless categories. Eventually, we had the entire rug around us covered with piles and were doing our own personal version of Twister — one foot carefully placed here, another there, bend and drop.

An hour after beginning, we surveyed each other across the sea of ephemera.

"Right! Good work, Gretchen. You start at that end and I'll start here. Meet you in the middle." My boss dropped to the floor cross-legged. I did the same more slowly and stretched out a hand for the nearest stack.

Somewhere, there was a needle hidden. Somewhere, an answer — or at least a clue — to the puzzle. Although the job appeared mind-numbing in scope, I knew I'd have to concentrate every moment. Keen wits, a sharp eye. I'd need both.

I glanced down. I held a pile of obituaries. Friends? Relatives? Business associates? I began to read.

It didn't take long to realize I'd need to keep some sort of notes. Taking a notebook from my desk, I wrote "obits" at the top of a page, then numbered each piece of paper in the pile. John looked over, nodded approvingly and began a notebook of his own.

The most interesting death notice belonged to the murdered man. I read it over twice. It made no mention of the Honeycutt connection, other than to state he was found dead on Honeycutt land. Not a word about the dead man's business with Henry Honeycutt. Odd, I thought. But perhaps that had not been common knowledge so soon after the murder. There were no survivors listed either. No grieving widow. No fatherless children. Truly a man alone.

"I've got financial records," John said, flapping a fistful of papers. "How about you?"

"Obituaries." I wrinkled my nose. "Pretty dreary stuff." I set them aside and reached for a more appealing-looking group.

The news clippings should reflect Henry's interests, I decided, giving me a strong feeling that they might hold the key. Shifting positions, I lifted the top sheet to catch the light.

A grainy photograph filled the top of the page, and I was surprised to recognize Bert and Doris at its center. The couple was dressed to the nines, Bert in a tuxedo complete with bow tie, Doris in a lacy evening gown. They were beaming at a man seen only in profile. Bert's hand was extended, ready to shake. It reminded me of a photo I'd once seen of the Duke and Duchess of Windsor meeting Hitler before the war. My eyes dropped to the caption.

"Present at Cross Company's gala event were Bert and Doris Honeycutt, seen here with Cross Company executive Jim Gallagher. The couple was instrumental in Cross Company's recent expansion into land development."

The rasp of my breath, sharply taken in, alerted John. "What?" he asked quickly, hopefully. "Have you found something?"

Awkwardly and with the grinding of knee joints, I got up without disturbing the carpet of paper surrounding me. "I don't know. Maybe!" I widened my eyes as I took big steps across the room. Even being very careful it was impossible to avoid crunching the documents underfoot, and I could only hope I didn't crinkle something valuable.

John took the paper I thrust at him.

"Look!" I pointed a finger at the smiling faces. "Bert and Doris." A pause. "Again."

John dropped his eyes, and I studied him. Oh, what a profile! I thought as a smile tugged at my lips. His cheeks were shadowed by whiskers, and there were fine creases at the corners of his eyes as he squinted at the poor quality photograph.

"First, Bert and Doris were the only other people on the estate at the time of the murder. Now, we have proof of them hob-nobbing with the dead man. I won't jump to any conclusions, John. But I wouldn't blame you if you did."

John gave a low chuckle, slipping his arm around my waist. "Very persuasive, Ms. Waller. Let's see if we can find any corroborating evidence, hmm?" He leaned over, and I closed my eyes, tilting my head to receive his kiss. His lips were soft and warm and seemed to draw me in. I pulled him closer as the kiss deepened. He felt so strong and firm beneath my hands, those broad shoulders able to take on the world.

When at last our mouths parted, I quipped, "That's some reward for just a clue. What do I get if I solve the crime?"

He squeezed me so tight my breath came out in a whoosh. "I think we could negotiate something," he promised, one eyebrow lifting in a way both suggestive and comical.

I laughed. "There's incentive! Back to work!"

By six o'clock, we had boiled down the project. Nearly all the papers went into file folders I labeled with their topic — finances, family, obituaries, and so on. The remaining stack, about three inches thick, represented every possible clue we could think of. It contained not only the murdered man's death notice but also all the news clippings related to the murder. John had tossed in records of financial transactions which Jim Gallagher had been a part of, although nothing specific to the real estate deal was found.

I sat back on my heels when that became apparent.

"Maybe Gramps didn't think they pertained to the case," John ventured. He rubbed his jaw with one long finger. He'd been handling old carbon paper copies, so the gesture left a smudge.

As I reached up to rub it off I suggested, "Or someone got to the safe before us."

John's hand moved quickly to capture my own, then raised it to his lips and kissed each knuckle in turn. "Impossible." Kiss. "Gramps is the only one who knows the combination." Kiss, kiss. "You have an overactive imagination." Kiss. "Too much reading." Lingering kiss, on my thumb.

I put my other hand against his chest to keep my balance. Was the room spinning, or was that my imagination, too?

A terse knock at the door successfully spoiled the mood.

"Supper's on the table," Al called out.

135

John sighed. "Duty calls."

Laughing, I took his hand, and we started toward the door — but not before putting the file folders back inside the safe and locking them in.

CHAPTER SIXTEEN

Dinner was a stilted, uncomfortable affair and with good reason. The threat of the pending interviews hung over the table, holding conversation to a minimum. For a time Doris made an effort, detailing the last vacation she and Bert had taken. But there was only so much she could say about Las Vegas — what they'd won, what they'd lost, what they'd eaten.

I made appropriate remarks of interest, remembering my new job assignment to be friendly.

Bert displayed a tendency to interrupt with his mouth full, correcting unimportant details in Doris' story. As the debate went on between them, I studied him across the table.

He ate like a condemned man, shoveling in forkfuls of potatoes until his round cheeks bulged. The ordeal of dinner made his complexion look ruddy and thoroughly unhealthy. My eyes darted away, down to my own plate. Suddenly, I wasn't very hungry.

By the time dessert was served — a sinful peach cobbler that revived my appetite — we had lapsed into silence. The clink of spoon against dish was the only sound to fill the room and soon grated on my nerves. Sighing, I squirmed in my seat, wanting the meal to be over. At the first opportunity, I made my escape, spending a few blissful moments of solitude before reconvening with the others in the library.

There, of course, things went from bad to worse. Bert and Doris didn't want to answer any questions of any sort. "And do you really need that?" Doris pointed one long fingernail at the old tape recorder on the desk. "I mean, honestly, John, you make me feel like a criminal."

"That isn't my intention, I assure you." He gestured to me, and I pushed the record button on the tape player. The soft, mechanical hum began, and John stated the date, the place and who was present.

"Let's set the scene," he said, the words soft, almost dreamlike. He sat on the edge of the desk, one leg dangling.

The room was dimly lit, curtains drawn against the cold night. The air was scented by Doris' perfume and the faded, woodsy aroma of Bert's pipe. I blinked, pushing myself upright in my chair. It would be easy to doze off, I knew, in the warm, darkened room and with a full tummy. I tuned back in to John's narrative.

"It's summer two years ago now. After an impromptu weekend house party, all the guests have gone." A pause. A direct look at Doris, then Bert. "All but two. You two. Gramps. Mary. Al. Five people in this entire house. Just five here when a murder takes place in the woods out there."

One finger jabbed in the direction of the window, and I shivered. The imagery was creepy, indeed.

"Gramps had gone out for a walk with Big Nick."

Lying on the rug at my feet, the dog pricked up his ears when he heard his name. His tail gave one big thump, and I reached down to pat him on the head. "Good boy," I whispered and was rewarded with another thump.

"Gramps told Gretchen and me earlier today he heard someone else in the woods while on that walk. Did he hear the murdered man — or the murderer?" John spread his hands, waiting for some sort of response.

Doris shifted, Bert drummed his fingers on the wooden armrest, Big Nick sighed deeply and closed his eyes.

"I don't know!" John continued. "But you might, and that's why we're here. To discuss your actions, your whereabouts, on that summer night two years ago."

"Should have gone on the stage, John. Your talents are wasted on me," Doris drawled. "It was a visit like any other." Her shoulders lifted and fell. "Bert and I sat in the garden. Perhaps we played croquet on the lawn. I probably read a book."

"Deadheading." Bert blurted the word and, for an instant, I didn't know what he was talking about. "I did some deadheading in the garden. A spot of weeding too, I believe. You know, Al doesn't keep up with that the way he should, John. It might be time to get a younger man in here."

"Could we stick to the subject, please? Al's doing the best he can, I'm sure." John steered the conversation back on track. "You worked in the garden in the afternoon?"

Bert nodded. "Until tea, I believe. Then," he crossed his arms over his chest. "I napped. I always nap in the late afternoon."

"That's true," Doris corroborated. "He does."

"Right. Then let's move on to the evening.

After dinner."

I leaned forward, checking the tape in the machine to be sure every word was recorded. There was still plenty of tape left.

"Well, what, Bert? I suppose we watched some television for a while," Doris said, one hand fiddling with the chain on her glasses. "But, see, I'm guessing now! I don't actually remember. Oh, this is ridiculous!"

It did seem pretty hopeless to me. I knew I could never recall what I'd done on a summer night two years ago. I bit my lip and thought. On the other hand, if a crime had taken place that same night, how could you <u>not</u> remember? There would have been police interviews, certainly. The scandal! The notoriety! Bert and Doris seemed like the type who would dine out on the story for weeks, regaling friends and innocent bystanders alike with their tale of horror.

"Allow me to refresh your memories." John slipped off the desktop and circled behind it. He made a production out of carefully producing a key to unlock one bottom drawer. Lifting a manila file folder out, he flipped it open, saying casually, "I have here a copy of your police interview, conducted the day the body was discovered."

Bert gave a start, and Doris gasped before asking, "How did you obtain those?"

Shaking his head, John said, "Oh, no. That's on a need-to-know basis and, frankly, you don't need to know."

Doris fumed. Bert blustered. John just kept shaking his head, the file folder of facts clasped firmly in his hand.

I wondered for a moment how he had gotten access to such information. Surely, the police wouldn't divulge all that! But, officially, the case was closed. There had been a conviction. The image of John's grandfather dressed in faded denims, elbows propped up on the table, popped into my mind. He had a nice smile and a friendly manner. Certainly not the stereotype of a murderer.

John withdrew a sheet of paper and began to read. " 'I retired to my room directly after dinner. My constitution is quite delicate, and I'm afraid the afternoon sun had brought on one of my sick headaches.' " He turned to Doris. "Accurate?"

She hooked one finger into the chain on her glasses and ran it up and down in what was obviously a nervous habit. "Yes," she said at last. "Now that you remind me, I do believe I did have a migraine. My grandmother had them, and you know they skip a generation —"

"So, you spent the entire evening in your

room and did not come down until morning?" John cut off her anecdote.

Doris nodded.

"And you were staying in which room?" His pen was at the ready to make a note of her answer.

"I was in Auntie's room." Her eyes darted over to me, spearing me with a look of irritation. "I always stay there. Except now, of course. You're there, Gretchen."

"Would you care to switch?" I asked. "It's no trouble at all. Although I will miss the ghost . . ."

"You've seen her?" Bert asked, sitting bolt upright, eyes bright with curiosity. "When? What did she —"

"I smelled her, actually," I clarified. "The scent of violets."

"Could we please get back to the matter at hand? Everyone can just stay where they are, and Gretchen can tell you all about the ghost and the violets later, okay?"

Bert caught my eye and pouted, full lower lip poking out. I shrugged and gave him the slightest of smiles to reveal my own disappointment. It would have been fun to discuss Auntie.

"So, you saw nothing unusual that night?" John pressed Doris.

"As I've said already, many times." She

tapped her toes against the rug. "I got up once to open the window, I think. It was a warm night." She paused, adding sarcastically, "But that should be in your notes, John."

He ignored her barb. "What about you, Uncle Bert? Where were you all evening?"

His uncle rubbed his palms together slowly, centering his concentration. "I, uh, I watched a movie in the front room. Then, went out on the lawn to smoke my pipe. Doris is right, it was a warm night. The air felt good."

"You went out on the back lawn, or the front?"

"Um, the back. I remember, because on my way in, I stopped off at the kitchen for a snack. Ice cream." He nodded proudly. That important detail had come readily to mind.

John consulted his notes. "It says here you heard something. What?"

Bert's eyes drifted toward the ceiling, then closed. "I . . . I heard a dog! Yes, I remember now. I heard the dog barking." He pointed at Big Nick, who slept on peacefully.

"Anything else?"

"Just a whistle. I'm assuming that was your grandfather, calling the dog."

Nodding in understanding, John asked, "And then, you came back in?"

"Ended up asleep in front of the television, I'm afraid."

"Hmm." John paced the room. "I'm assuming at some point you woke up and went up to bed."

"Doris woke me."

"What?"

"Doris woke me, around midnight or so?" Bert made his answer into a question.

I frowned, my gaze shifting from John to Bert to Doris. In that moment, I was infinitely glad I was a mere spectator at this event.

"I thought you were in your room all night with a headache." John directed his remark to Doris.

"Oh, I may have gotten up once or twice. I can't be sure," Doris was casual. "You know, I hope you've questioned Mary and Al so thoroughly."

But John stuck to his course. "So, you may or may not have been prowling around in your pajamas that night."

Knitting his brows, Bert's eyes grew thunderous. "I take offense at your tone, John. Doris was not prowling around," he quoted the words in a mincing voice. "And she was most certainly not in pajamas!" He thumped the arm of his chair.

Apparently, appearing in nightclothes was

a punishable offense in Bert's book. But that, of course, was not the point John leapt upon.

"Not in pajamas. In what, then? Suit and tie?"

Bert, realizing his gaffe, began backpedaling. "I cannot recall, umm . . ."

"Oh, Bert, be quiet!" Doris hissed. "You'll have him convicting me of murder in a minute."

Beneath her sharp gaze, Bert shifted and withered. There'd be an argument between them, I knew, as soon as they left this room.

"Doris, come clean." John's pen tapped rapidly against the desktop. "You're making this take twice as long as it has to. Just tell us where you went and why."

For a moment, I thought she wasn't going to answer. Then, I expected her to demand a lawyer. Instead, she gave a great sigh, taking strength from the gesture.

"All right. I had been outside. I woke up. It was late — near midnight — and the room was just so warm. I went over to open a window, and then I just stood there, letting the little bit of breeze blow over me. When I looked out over the lawn," she paused, on the brink of revelation, then rushed on. "I thought I saw something. Someone."

"Who?" I asked.

She gave a short laugh. "It was dark. The figure was at the edge of the lawn. There was no way to identify him from there. So I got dressed and went for a look."

"Wait a minute, wait a minute." John was incredulous. "You went out — alone — into the dark of night to look for a prowler?"

"Exactly. I am not some feeble old woman, John. Nor am I a fraidy cat. I was prepared. I was armed."

"Armed!" All three of us exclaimed at once.

"I had a flashlight. I had my pepper spray."

Bert's eyes stayed wide in amazement; John still looked quizzical. I had no trouble picturing this woman, self-sufficient and fearless, charging off into the unknown, fueled only by curiosity.

"Did you find the intruder once you were outside?" Me again, on the edge of my seat.

"Of course."

"Well, who was it? Why didn't you tell this to the police? It must have been the murderer!" I prattled.

Doris shifted in her seat, still twiddling with her eyeglass chain. "Well, I didn't speak to him, I'll tell you that. As soon as I recognized the man, I came back." She broke off, knowing the suspense in the room was palpable.

We let Bert ask the question.

"Who was it, dear?"

"Why, it was Al's brother, of course."

CHAPTER SEVENTEEN

"What?"

"No!"

"Don?"

The room filled with our excited, questioning voices. Doris took the time to look pleased with herself before answering.

"That's right. Don." She spoke his name as if it were a cuss word and shuddered ever so slightly. "I'm surprised your grandfather allowed that black sheep on his property."

John's mouth worked, holding back what would have been an angry retort. I jumped into the opening.

"Al has a brother?"

"Oh, yes. Don. Fancies himself some sort of wilderness man. Living off the land and all that sort of rubbish. Living off the generosity of others, if you ask me. In my day, we called them bums."

"Bit of a drifter, that man." Bert took up the tale. "Haven't seen him in years.

149

Thought he was dead, actually."

John took a deep breath in, his hands clasped tightly together. When he spoke, it was with infinite patience. "Doris, please tell me why you never mentioned Don's presence to the police during the investigation."

"Well, at first I held off because I knew it would look bad for Al," she said. "And I certainly didn't want to get him in trouble with his employer." Her voice sounded sincere, but I noticed John frowning. Sincerity, it would seem, was not Doris' strong suit.

"Anyway," she rushed onward, "I never expected your grandfather to get in trouble. I thought the police in this town would be capable of catching a criminal." Her snort of laughter was unseemly. "My mistake! By the time I could see which way the wind was going to blow, it was too late to come forward." Her eyes darted around the room. "I was afraid I'd be accused of obstructing justice or something. They might send me to jail!"

"So you let Gramps go instead, knowing he was innocent? How dare you?" There was a quaver in John's voice as he took rapid strides around the room, barely holding fury in check.

Doris had the good grace to look uncomfortable. Beneath the heavy layers of makeup, her skin went pale. Her fingers tapped a staccato rhythm against the arm of the chair, and she dipped her head, avoiding everyone's gaze. "You're right! You're right! It was a monstrous thing to do. But what can I say? I didn't have a choice."

"Oh, yes, you did —" John began, ready to rail at his aunt.

Such an attack struck me as pointless. Leaving my post by the recorder, I crossed the room to John's side and placed one hand gently on his shoulder. Squeezing, I said, "I'm sure Doris regrets her error in judgment. Why don't you have an officer stop out tomorrow, and take her statement? She'd be willing to cooperate, I'm sure." As I spoke, I looked to the woman in question and nodded.

"If I must," she said with great reluctance.

"You must." John was firm. He shook off my hand, but not before giving me a grateful look.

Doris pushed herself up from the chair. "If it's all the same to you, I'll retire to my room now." Her lips pursed. "All this dreadful talk has brought on one of my headaches." Fingers to her temples, she closed her eyes and winced.

"Yes, all right, whatever," John agreed, snapping off the recorder. "I think we've done all we can do here, anyway."

Bert did his best to leap to his feet and follow in his wife's wake. Even Big Nick rose, stretching his long legs and giving a mighty yawn.

"John," I began, but he cut me off.

"Not now, okay, Gretchen?" His eyes looked tired, red-rimmed and a little puffy. "I'm going to take Big Nick for a run."

The dog's ears pricked up when he heard his name, and he gave a short bark of anticipation. "You can join us if you like."

The invitation seemed sincere, but I begged off. "You two go ahead." I stroked Big Nick's chin, and his tail thumped in pleasure against my ankle.

I did go as far as the front door with them, kissing John after he had donned cap and gloves. When I moved away after the casual peck, he reached out, pulling me quickly against him for a more powerful, lingering embrace. His lips against mine were magic — warm and stirring and filled with unspoken promises.

One finger crept under my chin, gently caressing the delicate skin there. His mouth only inches from mine, John said, "One day all this darkness will be behind us, Gretchen."

"Yes." I reached up, twining my arms around his neck. "Yes," I repeated before our lips touched once more.

Big Nick decided he had been patient long enough and gave a low-throated, mournful whine of protest.

"He doesn't approve," I quipped, laughing.

John knelt to attach a long leash to the dog's collar. Looking up at me, he joked, "Ah, he's just jealous." He straightened up, gave me a wink, then headed out into the night.

CHAPTER EIGHTEEN

On my way to the main staircase, I paused to examine the photographs jamming the table against the wall. John had interrupted my earlier study on our first day at Mill Hollow, and I hadn't had a chance to return for a better look at the Honeycutts at play.

My eyes moved at once to the shot of John cannonballing. I smiled, extending a finger to touch the frame gently. Big Nick's picture had a prominent position near the center of the table. The picture showed the dog at his master's feet beneath a gnarly oak tree in autumn. Henry, John's grandfather, looked like a country squire in plaid flannel shirt and corduroys. One picture showed a huge Christmas tree filling the hallway where I now stood. One was of a family group out on the lawn.

I picked it up and brought it closer. There were at least fifty people in the photograph, arranged in three curving rows. It was summer, the lawn a deep green stretching to the ends of the picture. Looking for John, I realized this photo must have been taken the same day as John's swimsuit shot. There he stood, toward the end of the middle row, bare-chested and with something — a knotted beach towel, I presumed — draped around his neck. Peering more intently, I recognized Bert in fishing cap and Bermuda shorts. At his side stood Doris, the only person in long pants and a jacket. She stood with her shoulders hunched up as if she were cold. Still, she managed to look her own brand of stylish. The jacket was blue and suitably nautical, with brass buttons marching down the front. The sunshine caught the glint off the chain from her eyeglasses. It seemed that chain was an essential accessory. I wondered idly if she had ever lost it.

Setting the heavy frame back on the table, I turned toward the room Bert called the parlor, then stopped. What if Bert were in it? There had been too much sitting and talking, I decided. Too much conversation. Faced with those options, I knew what I longed for most of all — solitude. Peace and quiet. And perhaps a few bubbles. I trotted off to run a hot tub.

A few hours later, as I sat up in bed writing a gossipy letter to Sandy, I heard a persistent scratching at my bedroom door. While I puzzled over its source a high-pitched whine began to accompany it, and I leapt from my bed, tossing back the covers in a rush.

"Coming!" I called, undoing the lock and bending down low.

Just outside, waiting patiently, was Big Nick. He had tipped his head to one side, looking for all the world as if he were pondering a question. The tips of his ears flopped over in an adorable, thoroughly charming way.

I rubbed those ears, turning my face so he could lick my cheek. "Do you want to sleep in my room, big guy?" I asked. The question was moot; he was already moving past me into the room, sniffing around for the best place to sleep.

"Hope Auntie's ghost won't scare you," I went on. I closed the door, but didn't lock it, then climbed back beneath the covers.

Big Nick walked three times around in a tight circle, then collapsed onto the rug at the foot of the bed. The softest, deepest one. A whoosh of air came out as the dog gave a sigh of contentment. Within moments the gentle wheeze of his even breathing was the only sound. It was hypnotic, lulling me closer and closer to sleep. At last I tossed aside my letter and snapped off the light. Soon, I knew, I'd be wheezing, too.

Something cold and wet was pressed against my cheek, and I could feel that draft just whispering against my skin. I came awake in an instant, already sniffing for the scent of violets. All I got was a hair up my nose — a long, soft dog hair.

"Nick!" I sputtered, pushing the covers away. I'd forgotten the dog was camping out in my room and certainly hadn't been expecting his cold, wet nose to nudge me awake in the middle of the night. His tail smacked the bed rail a few times, and he gave a whimper. As I reached for the light switch, I heard one paw scrape down the bedroom door. Obviously getting out was a matter of some urgency.

Without bothering to retrieve my robe, I opened the door and watched Big Nick slip quickly into the shadowed hall, the tags on his collar chiming softly with each step. Would Mary or Al let him out, I wondered. What if they didn't awaken?

Crossing my arms over my chest, I moved

reluctantly away from the warm nest of my bed and down the chilly corridor. I could let the dog out for a potty stop, and we could both be back in bed in five minutes, I reasoned. At the top of the staircase, I was glad to see dim lights spaced along the baseboard. At least I wouldn't break my neck on this midnight run.

The tiled floor was icy beneath my bare feet, sending a shiver clear up my spine. Mill Hollow was rather eerie in the dead of night. The high ceiling swallowed any moonlight that might stream in, and every corner was engulfed in dark shadows. In the overwhelming silence, not a creature was stirring — except Big Nick and me.

I thought I could hear the click of Nick's toenails as he hurried down the hall to the back doors, so I turned in that direction. I hadn't gone far when I heard a door open and shut. Then came a whistle, short and sharp. Al, of course, out in the yard with the dog. My job was over before it began. I could go straight back to bed.

I took a step, stopped, then took another. Even though my bare feet made no sound on the tiles, I moved with caution, still going in the direction of the back doors.

When I was a few feet from the glass French doors, I stepped off to the side. It wouldn't do to have Al see me spying on him like some gothic heroine. Without slippers, in my long nightgown, all I needed to complete the image was a glowing candle.

A heavy silhouette passed the doorway, followed immediately by another just as big. I frowned. Who was accompanying Al? Mary? The idea seemed unlikely. Peering out, I saw Big Nick running over the snow, his nose down, sniffing the trail of a rabbit or some other nocturnal creature. Standing about twenty feet from the house, Al and — could it be? — Bert had their heads together in earnest conversation. Well, here was an interesting duo! I stepped closer to the glass, crossing my hands behind my back.

As I watched I could see Al knitting his brow. Bert was talking intently at him, rather than to him, rearing back a bit on his heels, then leaning forward to poke a finger in Al's direction. Al's mouth opened in a gasp, then he began to talk back, his cheeks puffing out in anger. If it hadn't been after midnight, they would have been shouting, I felt sure. Once, I saw Bert look over his shoulder at the house, as if he feared their altercation might awaken someone. Al, following his gaze, dropped his own decibel level as well.

Like a peeping Tom, I watched from the

shadows as the conversation escalated. The hand gestures grew more vivid, their facial expressions increasingly angry and determined. At last, Al pulled back an arm, and I winced, anticipating the blow, but at the last instant the caretaker caught himself. He waved Bert away in disgust, like an unwelcome ant at a picnic, and stalked off across the snow toward the dog. For a moment, I thought Bert might follow him. He watched Al head around the corner of the house, then I saw his shoulders lift and fall in a sigh of defeat. I knew his next move would be to turn in the direction of the French doors, so I hiked up the hemline on my nightgown and took to my heels, sprinting down that long hallway and up the winding stairway. I'd been safely in my room for a full five minutes before I heard Bert go past, betrayed by the creaking floorboards.

What could they have been talking about? Al's brother, of course, and Doris' damaging testimony. She'd all but said Al's brother was the real murderer.

Just before I closed my eyes, I wondered if it would be safe for Doris and Bert to eat the food prepared by Mary. Perhaps they would be wise to hire a taster if Mary was as angry as Al.

CHAPTER NINETEEN

At breakfast the next morning it seemed Bert was sliding his eggs around a bit more than necessary, and I figured he was searching for ground glass. I didn't really think Al or Mary would cause him harm, but it seemed obvious the thought had crossed Bert's mind. Eventually, he stopped poking and, deeming them safe, tucked into his scrambled eggs with great enthusiasm.

I took a seat beside Doris and gave them both what I hoped was an encouraging smile. John sat on the opposite side, hidden behind the bulk of the morning paper.

"Isn't it a frosty one?" I said, gesturing out the window at the sunny winter day.

I'd wrapped up against the cold in a pair of baggy green corduroys, a black turtleneck and a lighter green cardigan with big patch pockets. Truly, the country look.

Doris looked up from her plate and smiled in polite acknowledgement. John gave me a wink; Bert merely kept eating.

So much for conversational forays, I thought, reaching for the coffee pot.

I had barely finished breakfast when the door to the dining room burst open to reveal an anxious Al. His eyes scanned the table, and he headed over to John, already talking.

"Mary's broken her tooth — pretty badly, I'm afraid. I've called the dentist in town, and he can see her this morning, but we'll have to leave at once."

John set aside his newspaper, his face the picture of concern. "Of course, Al. Take as long as you need." He made a shooing motion with his hands.

Al bobbed his head once and hurried from the room. He didn't even seem to realize other people sat around the table. All his thoughts seemed focused on Mary. A moment later, the faint sound of a door closing indicated their departure.

"That's too bad," I said. "Al looked awfully concerned. I hope he remembers to wear his seat belt and drive safely. They left in such a rush."

"Probably left the oven on," Doris commented acidly. "Big emergency." She picked at a piece of grapefruit with her fork.

I frowned. Really, she was a very callous

woman. It was difficult to like her.

Across the table, John sighed and pushed back his chair. "That will do, Doris." He didn't see her scrunch up her nose in distaste at his reprimand.

I tossed my napkin onto the table and followed John out. In the hallway, we exchanged a look of exasperation. Before either of us could speak, the sound of toenails clicking on the tile announced the arrival of Big Nick. The dog made a beeline for John, sitting at his feet and looking up mournfully.

"Hey, old man," John greeted him, patting the dog soundly on the back.

Big Nick responded with the same high-pitched keening I'd heard the night before in my bedroom.

With a glance at his watch, John said, "Well, it's time for your morning constitutional, isn't it? Al left in such a hurry, he forgot about your walk!" He turned to me. "Wanna come along?"

"Lead the way!"

Inside of five minutes we were bundled up for the great outdoors. Bert and Doris had been given orders to clean up the breakfast dishes, and John's step was light as we started out. Big Nick had been on his leash, but John quickly unsnapped it so the dog could run. It was a joy to see him enjoying himself, moving easily through the snow on his powerful legs while John and I trailed far behind. The sight sparked the memory of my midnight rendezvous. In a few words, I related the story to a quizzical John.

He listened with great interest, then pushed both gloved hands through his hair and growled a little.

"I am so sure all the answers to this mystery are right here, right now, if only everyone would confess their secrets!"

"Fat chance of that."

"Gramps already gave me the answer. Something from the safe must hold the key," John went on as if I hadn't spoken. He blinked, bringing me into focus. "That's the first order of business this morning, Gretchen. As soon as we're back . . ."

His thought was cut off by the sudden staccato barking of Big Nick. We were into the woods by now, the same woods I'd wandered through on my very first walk here. The woods with eyes — or so I'd felt then.

"Nick?" John called, then gave a whistle.

The barking went on, unabated. The dog sounded more frantic now — excited, not panicky.

Our eyes met in question. "Probably just

164

a squirrel or something," I suggested hope-fully.

Shaking his head, John took off at a trot. "You know, it wasn't too far from here that —"

"I know, I know. Don't remind me!" I kept pace beside him, hoping we weren't about to make a gruesome discovery of our own.

It was a discovery all right, but not the kind I'd been fearing.

Big Nick stood alternately barking and whining at the back of his throat, his eyes trained steadily on a person I had never seen before. The old man stood about six feet from the dog, his back up against the wall of a little wood cabin. He was effectively trapped.

John stopped so abruptly at the sight that I smacked into him hard. He didn't seem to notice.

"Well, I'll be . . ." I heard him say softly before stepping forward. "Good boy, Nick." John walked up to the dog and gave him a pat. The dog looked to John then, but John had turned his attention to the stranger.

The old man was tall and rangy, with a long, snowy beard and shoulder-length hair. His face was thin and deeply wrinkled. Puffy bags beneath his eyes made him look tired, but his expression was one of curiosity. Heavy white eyebrows, so bushy they appeared to be one continuous line, lifted in question as the man looked to John.

"H-hello," he greeted us, and I could see his shoulders relax a bit.

John didn't waste time on pleasantries. "Do you think you could tell me what you're doing here? This is private land." He glanced to the open cabin door. Inside, a wooden table scattered with dishes was visible. A faint smell of bacon still hung in the air.

Shifting from one foot to the other, the old man shrugged. His thin flannel shirt couldn't be keeping him warm in the cold morning air, and his jeans were worn white at the knees. Only his boots, sturdy hiking boots with thick treads, seemed adequate in the temperature.

"Your grampa never minded if I stayed. Reckon he wouldn't mind now, iffen you'd ask him." The speech was soft and unhurried.

Standing off to the side as an observer, I blinked. He knew Henry. He knew John. He knew —

"Does Al know you're here? Does Mary?" John's question provided me with an answer. Al's brother, the wanderer. The — what had Doris said? — "wilderness man."

"Of course they do, John. Can't say I'll be here much longer, though. Doesn't pay to get too settled." He rubbed gnarly, arthritic fingers up and down his arms. "We gonna stand here talking all day or can we move this chat inside. I've got some coffee left." The perfect host, he gestured to the open door.

I glanced to John, and he gave a nod, tipping his head to indicate I should precede him. Two shallow wooden steps led up to the door, and I noticed they had been carefully cleared of snow and ice. Propped next to the doorway an obviously old and well-cared-for metal detector stood ready for use.

Inside all was tidy as well. An old-fashioned black iron stove held a skillet with the remains of breakfast. A pitcher of orange juice sat in the middle of the wooden table next to a stick of butter on a green-and-white-checked plate with a chip at one edge. I noticed there were toast crumbs on the old man's breakfast plate, but none on the stick of butter. Very, very tidy.

John pulled out a wobbly wooden chair and gestured me into it. Then, he sat down beside me on another equally rickety chair with Big Nick at his feet. The dog sat, stood, then crossed the room with an air of determination. I watched with interest as he sniffed cupboard doors, finally choosing one to sit in front of, his eyes boring into the wood.

Al's brother, Don, carried his breakfast plate to the long sink under one window, rinsed it carefully and set it on the drain board before addressing Big Nick.

"So, now you remember, hmm? You've been here before, for sure. You remember me?" He squatted down in a slow, painful-looking process to rub the dog's neck, his fingers working under the heavy leather collar. The familiar sound of Big Nick's tail smacking wood came next, followed by his trademark high-pitched whine.

"He wants whatever is in that cupboard," I said, brilliant in my deduction.

"He surely does," Don agreed, opening the door and pulling out a package of leathery-looking beef jerky. "I always have a little of this stuff on hand. Tastes awful, but it's handy. Old Nick's a big fan of it, though, aren't you, buddy?" Holding out one long piece, he gave it a wiggle beneath the dog's quivering nose. Big Nick's mouth opened wide, and the beef jerky disappeared.

I laughed out loud at the display, and even John seemed to sense the affection the old man had for the old dog.

168

"I haven't been around here for quite some time. Glad to see the dog's still around, even if it took him a while to know me. Must be the beard threw him off. Didn't have it the last time through."

"When would that have been?" John asked.

"I'm forgetting my manners! Would you like some coffee? Plenty left." Don indicated the old-fashioned coffee pot, blue-speckled and dented.

John shook his head. I couldn't turn down such generosity and smiled. "Yes, please."

In a moment, Don was back with a ceramic mug filled to the brim with deep brown liquid. I took a sip, expecting the worst and was pleasantly surprised. My expression must have been revealing because Don grinned at me, nodding his head slowly and saying, "I make a fine cup of coffee, miss. One of my most important survival skills." He surprised me then by giving me a saucy wink.

When he turned back to John, however, he grew somber. "So, you'll be tossing me out of here, I take it." He lifted broad, thin shoulders. "Your decision, of course. And it's probably time I moved on anyway. Haven't been here over long, though. Not more than a week or two." He extracted a pocket watch on a long, shiny chain, glanced at the time, then returned it to his pocket. "Maybe three. Your grampa never minded me visiting," he repeated his earlier remark. "In fact, he used to say he wished he could join me."

"Really?" John sounded surprised.

"Uh huh. He'd come and set with me in the evenings and we'd build a fire if it was cool or stay outside if it was warm. 'Don,' he'd tell me. 'You're a lucky man. Not tied down. Free as the wind.' Yessir, he's a fine man, your grampa." Now, Don shook his head, and the morning sunlight made his white hair gleam.

Doris thought this man was the real murderer. After ten minutes in his company, I didn't think that was possible, but then, none of the people I'd met seemed capable of murder.

John began fishing for information. "I'm glad Gramps has good friends like you. He needs all the support he can get right now."

Don took a cautious sip from his own coffee mug. "There ain't no way that man took another life. He doesn't have it in him. It's that simple."

"Which brings me to my next question." John leaned forward, elbows on the table. "Do you?"

For a moment, I thought Don wasn't going to reply. His eyes darkened, and his eyebrows dropped down almost into them. I could see a muscle tighten in his cheek as he clenched his jaw. "Just what are you implying, sir?"

"I think I've said it, Don."

A long silence stretched further and further, like a rubber band ready to snap. I leaned back in my chair, out of harm's way if fists or fur started to fly.

"You're crazy, man, if you're thinking I did it."

John's look didn't waver. "Tell me what you know about the night of the murder, Don. You were on the grounds. You must have heard something. Seen something. Twigs snapping, maybe."

Don's mouth twisted with humor. "City slicker," he chided, not unkindly. "Did you read that in a book somewhere?" He chuckled, and it sounded like water bubbling over rocks.

John waited in silence. I concentrated on tracing the grain on the wooden table and watching the sunlight catch the links of Don's watch chain. Eventually, Don continued.

"I saw your granddad the night before I left." He nodded. "The night of the murder.

171

He and Big Nick stopped by during their walk. We talked a bit. Had a drink, maybe two. They didn't stay long. See, that's why I didn't give it any thought when I heard people later. Figured he'd met up with somebody from the house. The place was crawling with relatives, like every summer."

"No." I spoke instinctively, shaking my head. "Everyone but Bert and Doris had gone home. There were only five people in the house. Remember?" Arching my eyebrows, I waited for John to confirm my words.

He bobbed his head and lifted one hand, covering his mouth in concentration.

Don frowned and when he did, his resemblance to Al became quite clear. The same no-nonsense expression, same creases between the eyes, same forbidding countenance. "Well, there was somebody out there in the woods. Man and a woman. Started out friendly, but then one of them got ornery."

"What were they arguing about? What did they say?" It was hard to keep from bouncing in my seat.

"They were a ways off, I couldn't hear the actual conversation," he said the word slowly, one syllable at a time. "Just the tone."

"What did you do when the yelling

started?" I asked, knowing full well what I would have done. Namely, prick up my ears and strain to make out every word.

Don turned to face me, planting his elbows firmly on the table. "I came inside and shut the door behind me, of course. Wasn't any of my business, was it?"

Point taken, I shrunk to mouse size.

"Besides, I had to pack up my stuff. Went off to Canada the next morning. Just got back."

"There's no chance you recognized the voices?"

Don's lips worked into something not quite a smirk. "The gal sounded familiar. But not the gent. Still, like I said, I couldn't hear them. Can't say anything I'd swear to in court."

Sitting back, John drummed his palms on the edge of the desk. "That's that, then."

"Yep."

At the door, the two men shook hands, and I knew a bargain was sealed. John wouldn't make Don leave his little cabin in the woods, now or ever. For his grandfather's sake.

The cold air felt wonderful after being tucked up in the tiny cabin. I glanced at the old metal detector.

"Do you find anything much with this?" I

asked, curious. "You know, valuable?"

Don cocked his head. "I'm bettin' your idea of valuable is a sight different from mine." Then, he smiled. "Found a silver fork once. Genuine silver. Last week, I found this chain." He pulled out the watch and displayed the length of gold. "Shined up nice. Not real gold, but it does the job right."

"I guess you never know what you'll find," I said.

"That's a fact," Don gave my remark the attention it deserved.

Big Nick gave an impatient bark, and I sketched a wave to the old man. With Big Nick leading the way, we headed back to the house. Our feet made the snow squeak as we trekked along. I left John alone with his thoughts for a moment.

When I couldn't stand it any more, I said, "At least now we know the murderer is a woman."

John blinked, coming back from a million miles away. "I guess that's so."

"Guess? It seems obvious. A man — the victim — and a woman — the killer." I spread my arms wide to emphasize the simplicity of it all.

"Sounds too simple," John said, maddeningly.

I lifted my shoulders and shivered just a little. "Maybe it is simple — that part. Still doesn't answer the who part."

"Narrows it down a bit, though."

"Down to two. Mary and Doris."

"Doris is a shrew." John's assessment was frank. "But being disagreeable doesn't make you a criminal."

"True." There was no other possible response. "That leaves — Mary?" I pictured the woman I knew where I knew her — at the stove, stirring a pot of thick stew and smiling.

John must have held a similar image.

"How?" he asked. "How can it be?"

We walked the rest of the way home in silence, and my mind drifted off to other things. I was scanning the treetops for cardinals when John stopped so abruptly I bumped into him.

"Now what?" he asked, looking toward the house.

A police car was parked out front.

CHAPTER TWENTY

"Well, John, I was just following orders," Doris said in an overly warm tone. "Your orders, in fact. 'Tell the police about Don,' you said." She shifted, crossing one plump leg over the other and looking triumphant.

Two uniformed officers had just left after speaking with Doris for nearly an hour. Poor Bert had spent the time pacing outside the closed door of the parlor as if he were expecting Doris to deliver more than simply information.

John's curiosity had been piqued, but he'd refused to indulge it, so I did, scurrying down the hall to ask Bert for the details.

He tossed his hands in the air. "Crazy idea! After all this time! Cops won't care! Henry should just . . . just take his punishment!" He'd sputtered the last. "And if he's not guilty of the murder, well, I'm sure he's guilty of something!"

Now, Bert leaned over to pat Doris' hand

in a soothing gesture. She fiddled with her eyeglass chain and thanked him with a smile. Her lips, blood red, pursed tightly, creating a network of lines around her mouth as Doris tipped her head to Bert. With a grunt, he hefted his torso over the arm of his chair, neck stretched out. His lips were so severely puckered, they stuck out a good two inches from the rest of his face. Their kiss when it came was noisy and brief. A stage kiss with John and me as the audience. But their eyes held in a manner of genuine affection that was difficult to fake.

Bert said, "I was so worried, Dorrie. You're very brave, my dear."

John turned away from the tender tableau, crouching down to pat the stretched-out length of Big Nick, who gave him an appreciative sigh. I, however, remained transfixed. Such enduring love is rare and, coming from this unlikely couple, even verged on the amazing.

"What did the police think of your story? Were they planning to question Don as a suspect?" John shoved his hands deep in his pants pockets and wandered over to the window.

"Far be it from me to second-guess the police, John. They just wrote down everything I told them and said they would be looking into it." Doris dismissed the incident with a wave of her bejeweled hand. "So, I've done my civic duty," she concluded in a smug tone.

"And now the spotlight will shine on Don." John's statement brought only a shrug from Doris.

"Where Dorrie says it belongs, young man," Bert said, raising one fist into the air. "That'd be a fine way to repay a friendship, if he's letting your grandfather pay for his crimes!" Bert's nostrils flared, and his skin took on an even more ruddy tone.

I glanced at John, but he had turned back to the window, pressing his forehead against the cool glass.

"Murder will out," I said simply, looking from John's tense shoulders to where Bert and Doris sat without moving. "Won't it?"

I took my work to bed with me that night. With John's permission, I had snatched up the folder of possible clues, telling him, "It will help me sleep."

His chuckle was sincere. "You mean it will put you to sleep!"

Hand in hand we mounted the heavy wooden staircase, the steps creaking softly. Parting when we reached the top, John reminded me, "I'll be right down the hall if you need me."

I nodded. "I know."

But he wasn't finished. "I mean, if you make a discovery that can't wait until morning. Or if Auntie pays you another ghostly visit."

He was joking now, so I wagged a finger under his nose. "Don't laugh! Maybe I'll just send her down the hall to you!"

He caught me close for a hug, then stepped on my foot.

"Nick!"

A glance down revealed not John's foot on mine, but the dog's. He had come soundlessly up the steps after us and now firmly declared his allegiance.

"Looks like he wants to stay with you tonight. Do you mind?"

I scratched the big dog behind the ears, and he looked up at me with liquid brown eyes. "Who could say no to that face?" I cooed as Big Nick's tail beat a tattoo against the rug.

"Softie." John's voice was a caress.

"That's me."

Big Nick brought the conversation to a halt by shaking his head to set his tags jangling, then marching off in the direction of my room.

"Good night, John!" I called over my shoulder, following the dog down the long, dark hall.

Clad in my fuzzy flannel nightgown, I climbed into bed in my usual pose, my knees propping up the folder of clues. If I looked through all this just before sleeping I reasoned, perhaps I'd find the answer in a dream. Stranger things had happened.

My tape player filled the air softly with classical, introspective music as I flipped through the newspaper scraps, rereading Jim Gallagher's obituary and all the news stories pertaining to the murder. I even turned the clippings over to see if anything printed on the other side might be important. But, no. That is, nothing obvious leapt out at me.

Big Nick, after settling on the rug, abruptly changed his mind and jumped onto the bed. He circled three times slowly, then collapsed into a tightly curled ball of fur, nose resting on paws.

I didn't draw the heavy curtains that night. The moon was full and shone off the snow bathing the room in diffused silver light. After a half hour or so of perusing the contents of the file folder I gave up, dropping it onto the floor next to the bed. Time for sleep, and plenty of it.

Hours later, I rolled over, and the light that had been lovely and romantic earlier poked me right in the eye. If anything, the moon was higher, delivering a piercing blaze, or so it seemed. It took only seconds for me to realize I'd have to draw the curtains after all.

At the foot of the bed, pinning my legs down, Big Nick wheezed quietly. Gently so as not to disturb him, I slid first one leg and then the other free of his weight and slipped from beneath the covers. The air felt cool after the warm cocoon of bed, so I moved with some speed to the window. Just before I yanked the cord, I detected the faint odor of violets in the room.

"Not tonight, Auntie," I pleaded, twitching my nose.

Drawing the drapes, I saw the room plunge into darkness and, with my hands stretched out in front of me, headed blindly back to bed.

The pain when it came was sharp and sudden, causing me to gasp in a breath and jerk my foot off the ground. I gave a curse and rubbed my bruised flesh. What had I stepped on? One of Big Nick's bones? A shard of glass?

I bent my knees and felt around, running

my hands over the rug. In seconds, I had found it — something round and smooth around the edges, but sharp on the top. Whatever it was, it could wait until morning. I tossed it into the empty water glass on my nightstand and scooted back into the welcoming nest of my bed.

The dog was my alarm the next morning. I let him out into the hall and he took off like a shot down the steps. It was as I pulled the cord to open the drapes that I remembered the piercing ache I'd felt after stepping on that thing in the night. Curious now to see my tormentor, I snatched up my water glass and held it up to the light.

At the bottom, swaying slightly from side to side, was a small brass button.

CHAPTER
TWENTY-ONE

It was only about an inch around, with a raised design on the top and a brass loop at the back for attaching it to a garment. The design was abstract, sort of vines and flowers. A woman's button, then.

Setting the glass down, I fished the button out, holding it in my palm at eye level. How on earth had it mysteriously appeared on my bedroom floor? Intruder? Why had I smelled the ghost's presence just before literally stumbling on this? Still in a foggy, just-from-sleep spell, I wondered if John's long-gone relative had provided me with a clue.

I deposited the button back in the glass for safekeeping and decided I'd withhold my thanks for later. As I dressed for another hard day at the office, the image of the button danced in my mind. It seemed familiar somehow, but I was almost positive it didn't belong to me.

Zipping up the side of my skirt, I mentally ran through my wardrobe. Holding my shoes in one hand, I crossed to the heavy armoire and flipped through the garments hanging there. No, not a brass button in sight.

I let my shoes clatter to the floor, tipping them upright with my toes and stepping into them. They were butter-soft brown flats that went well with the camel brown skirt which fell straight down from the hip. I'd chosen a patterned turtleneck to wear with it, adding a pin at the throat for an accent. After whisking a brush through my hair, I pulled it back into a ponytail with a tortoiseshell barrette, then added small gold button earrings and just one spritz of perfume. There!

The stair banister was smooth and cool beneath my hand as I skipped down the steps to breakfast. Maybe it was the sunshine making my heart light. Maybe the prospect of seeing John. I'd dreamt of him the night before. We'd been in a building with many corridors branching off to the vanishing point in every direction. The walls of the corridors were lined with doors. Closets, actually. In my dream, we'd been in a hurry to head off somewhere, but I couldn't leave because I didn't have my jacket. The entire dream consisted of me opening and closing closet doors while John stood behind me saying, "Come on! Come on!" It was like an old Keystone Cops film. The dream probably held all sorts of ominous portents for my future, but it was easy to ignore them just now.

I laughed at the remembered image. Big Nick had awakened me before I had found my jacket in the dream. If I fell asleep right now, I wondered, would I be searching for it still?

At the bottom of the stairway, I turned in the direction of the dining room and had gone past the table of photographs when a sudden thought brought me up short. Even the smell of pancakes drifting down the hall didn't urge me forward.

Stretching out a hand, I retrieved the family group shot from the table and peered closely over the people. Where, oh, where . . . Yes! There! There she stood, Aunt Doris, in her blue jacket — with brass buttons. If my hand shook slightly as I turned the frame over, I didn't notice it. It was the work of a moment to slide open the back of the picture frame, revealing the spidery, handwritten notation. "Fourth of July," it read, followed by the year. Two years ago, I thought. This photograph was taken on a summer weekend two years ago. Just days before the murder took place. Doris had had a jacket with bright brass buttons then. Did she have it still? Thoughtfully, I closed the back of the frame, pondering.

"Good morning, Gretchen."

The woman herself spoke from just a few feet away, standing alone at the base of the stairs, her fingers wound around her eyeglass chain.

I'm sure the start I gave looked guilty. I glanced hastily from her to the photograph I held, then set the frame down too fast, so it shoved a few others aside with a clatter.

"Hello, Doris. I was just going to breakfast."

Doris let her eyes travel slowly from my face to the photo and back again. "Really? It looked like you were doing more of your . . . research." She let me stand there wordlessly before going on. "Planning to put yourself in the family picture?"

My spine straightened at her words and their implication. I widened my eyes and put ice into my tone. "I'm sure I don't know what you mean."

Her laughter was brittle. "And I'm sure you do." She moved off the stairs and past me. "But that's fine, dear. You'll do John a world of good. He needs a steady influence. Much too excitable."

The heels of her shoes snapped a rhythm as she walked. I made a face at her back, then followed along.

Had Doris been in my room, snooping, and pulled a button loose? Had she lost the button on one of her previous visits? She had made it quite clear she usually stayed in my room.

As if she could hear my thoughts, Doris turned, looking over her shoulder at me in an assessing manner. There in the doorway of the dining room, our eyes locked. If judgment was in hers, accusation was in mine.

With my heart thudding in my ears I pushed by her, seeking the haven of my chair at the breakfast table.

John spared me a glance from behind the wall of newspaper. "What's up?"

I shook my head so briskly my earrings swayed. Placing my linen napkin in my lap, I said, "Later."

Lifting his coffee cup, John eyed me over its rim.

I wanted to tell him my theory. I wanted to hear him laugh it off. I wanted to show him the brass button and the photo of his aunt wearing a jacket with brass buttons. I wanted to remind him of his grandfather's story — the figure in a dark coat with something shiny on the front. I wanted to ask him if he thought the chain on Don's pocket watch — the chain he found last week on the estate — could be one of Doris' eyeglass chains. I wanted to have him see the picture of Doris and the dead man and leap, as I had, to a stunning conclusion.

Doris was the killer.

CHAPTER
TWENTY-TWO

Doris had known the dead man, as evidenced by the pictures. She and Bert looked pretty cozy with him in that shot, and we had surmised their involvement with the failed enterprise. An enterprise which brought shame and scandal to the Honeycutt family, the one thing Henry Hanover Honeycutt had always wanted to avoid. How angry had he been at the ruinous business? More importantly, how angry did Doris think he would be?

I looked up from my toast to find Doris watching me, her own fork held stiffly at attention. Position was everything to her. She was proud to be a Honeycutt and, no doubt, pleased with the comfortable lifestyle the name afforded her.

Had she met Jim Gallagher in the woods, perhaps, to discuss their mutual financial disaster? Had she made a suggestion — no, a demand — and been rebuffed?

The thought of Doris angry and feeling betrayed was enough to make me drop my toast. It hit the handle of my fork, sending it catapulting off the table onto the floor between John and me. We both leaned down to get it, our heads momentarily beneath the tabletop.

"Butterfingers," John chided gently.

But I was in no mood for teasing. "It's Doris," I hissed, my teeth clenched so hard I heard my molars grind. "The murderer! Doris!" To emphasize my point, I drew my finger over my throat.

John handed me the fork, his eyebrows furrowing into one solid, fuzzy line, incredulous.

I just nodded, and we both straightened up. John's eyes went at once to his aunt, who now sat placidly beside his uncle, the two of them sharing the last of the orange marmalade. When he glanced at me, I looked him smack in the eye and tried to send my message telepathically.

Yes! I wanted to shout. She had motive — fear of losing her father-in-law's favor. She had opportunity — there was photographic proof of her being on the estate, plus her own testimony of seeing a figure on the lawn after midnight and going to investigate. She had means — any old log in the woods would have done the job of knocking Gallagher unconscious. And once he was down . . . I shut my eyes at the image of Doris' ringed fingers pressing into a man's throat in rage.

"Excuse me." My voice was weak, and my stomach felt like a clenched fist, tense and strained. The chair pressed into my calves as I rose quickly and made for the door. Just a little fresh air, I thought. That's all I need. So, I stood on the little flagstone path just beyond the French doors, my arms crossed over my chest for warmth, breathing deep and slow and even.

No one came looking for me to see how I was, and I was grateful for that. With a few minutes alone, I could formulate a plan of some sort, couldn't I?

Of course, the logical thing to do would be drive straight to the police department and tell them my suspicions, explain my meager proof.

"And that's what I'll do!" I said the words aloud. I'd go to my room and retrieve the button, then get John to drive into town with me, straight to the cops.

The doorknob rattled as I shut the door and was engulfed by the warmth of central heating. As I passed the dining room, I could hear Doris and Bert talking. Good!

Big Nick was curled in a ball on a rug at the foot of the stairs, an effective roadblock. Just after I awkwardly stepped over him, he stood, stretched, and followed me up the carpeted stairs, a strong, firm presence at my side.

"Now, we're not up here for a nap, big guy," I chattered nervously as we entered my room. "We'll just get this button," I said. "Then, John and I will go off to fetch the police!"

As I talked I moved rapidly around the bed, past the window. I could see Al's ladder propped against the frame outside, but he was nowhere in sight.

At the night table, I shook the little button out of the glass I'd tossed it into last night. It felt light in my hand, far lighter than an object with such a dark history should, it seemed. For a long moment, I looked down at the button, as if I expected it to burn my skin. Then, before my nerve failed me, I curled my fingers tightly around it until its edges cut into my palm and turned to leave.

"All right, Big Nick, let's —"

At the instant I saw her, framed in the doorway, I heard Nick's low, guttural growl. A ridge of dark fur stood up on his spine, and his body was stiff with attention.

Doris, for her part, looked unconcerned. She leaned against the door jamb, one finger sliding up and down the chain on her eyeglasses. In her navy and white coatdress, she looked like an executive secretary, not a murderer.

"And what do you have there, Gretchen?" Her voice was slippery with sweetness and condescension. "Whatever have you found?"

Trapped at the far side of my room by the windows, it was easy to see there would be no escaping confrontation. My mouth was suddenly dry, and my tongue stuck to my teeth. I felt my limbs trembling ever so slightly, with fear and with adrenalin both. Wordlessly, I held out my hand and very slowly opened my fingers to reveal the button nestled there.

"I can't see," Doris whined and attempted to step into the room. Big Nick growled deeper, louder, standing his ground between us and earning my eternal gratitude.

Doris glared at him and hissed, "That dog is a nuisance. With Henry gone now, he should be put down before he bites someone!"

Her words, so selfish, so bitter, gave me courage and helped me find my voice. "Put down, Doris?" I put sarcasm into the euphemism. "Has it become so easy for you to kill?"

Her eyes flashed dark with anger, then she blustered, "Oh you wretched girl! What are you talking about? You speak such nonsense!" Another contemptuous glance at Big Nick. She took two steps into the room.

Nick retreated two steps, but still seemed cocked and ready to attack.

"Good boy! Good Nick!" I praised him, suddenly feeling I had the upper hand. I had my suspicions and what I considered evidence. But I also had John downstairs, aware of my ideas and, after all this while, wondering where I might be. At least I hoped he'd come looking for me soon. He had to!

John, I thought hard, get up here!

Doris wagged her pudgy fingers, the morning sun making the gems in her rings sparkle. "Come on, now. Let me see!"

"No." I was feeling contrary now. "But I'll tell you what it is, and you tell me where it came from."

Doris gave a sigh of exasperation.

"Button, button. I've got a button," I said, repeating the singsong of childhood in a deadly serious tone.

"Is that all?" Doris almost laughed. "All this drama because of a button? Well, you just keep it, dear." She pivoted on one chunky heel, as if to leave.

When she had her back to me, I pushed the "record" button on my tape player. Then, I spoke again.

"It's from your blue blazer," I stated. "The one you were wearing on the night you killed Jim Gallagher."

That got her attention.

"I don't own a blue blazer. You're wrong."

"Well, you did then. Dark blue. You're wearing it in the photograph downstairs. The one taken the day before the murder."

I could see the light of recognition flare briefly in Doris' eyes, and knew she was recalling that picture, that day.

"Yes," I said, nodding in confirmation. "Later that night, after all the others were gone, you met Jim Gallagher in the woods." When Doris did not respond, I hurried on, recounting the scenario as I'd constructed it. "You said you had a headache, so no one would disturb you. Bert was asleep in front of the television. Did he know what you were up to?"

I saw her start to shake her head, then abruptly stop the motion. "What is this? Some dream you had?" Her eyes narrowed dangerously. "Or has John the genius been feeding you these crazy ideas?" A smirk of disgust tugged at one ruby lip.

"Bert didn't know," I guessed, making the words a statement rather than a tentative suggestion. But he couldn't have known, I determined. He would never be able to feign ignorance as he'd done. His eyes and expression were too open, too guileless. With Bert, what you saw was what you got. "And, if Bert didn't know of your plan to commit murder, it must be because he didn't know something else." Rubbing my thumb over the pattern on the button, I kept my gaze trained on Doris standing stiffly in the doorway.

If I were wrong, she could just turn on one heel and walk away. If I were right, she'd need to know how much I'd pieced together. She'd stay to hear it all. Every second she stood there lent credence to my musings. It also increased the chances John would show up.

John, I thought fiercely, furrowing my brow, *get your nose out of that newspaper now!*

"You and the dead man were lovers?" I guessed and was rewarded with a quick burst of laughter. "Well, Doris, there is only love and money. So, if not love, then . . ." My voice trailed off, suggesting the obvious.

"What, Gretchen?" Crossing her arms

over her chest, she waited.

My brain whirled, swirling around the information I'd read in the files from the safe. "There was a photograph of you and Bert with Gallagher. The caption made it pretty plain you two were instrumental in bringing Gallagher and Henry Honeycutt together."

Across the room, Doris was motionless, her nonchalant stance voided by the intensity of her gaze.

From the corner of my eye, I caught a glimpse of the manila file folder of clues I'd dropped beside the bed the night before. The sight of it emboldened me, and I hurried on, bluffing wildly.

"And, of course, those papers we found make it all pretty clear." I snapped my fingers, almost smiling. "The bad real estate deal — the one which brought yet another scandal to the Honeycutt name —" I paused for dramatic effect, then pointed directly at her — one long finger of accusation. "It was all your idea!"

CHAPTER
TWENTY-THREE

"What?" Doris' voice had the high-pitched squeak of false denial. I saw her eyes dart swiftly over to the heavy dresser, then back to me.

I gasped, seeing everything, so suddenly, so clearly. "The papers were right in this room, the room you always stayed in here. You cooked up the whole real estate scheme. You thought it would be a moneymaker. You had no idea it would turn out so disastrously."

"No, you're wrong!" Stepping into the room, Doris drew back one well-shod foot as Big Nick approached her, his fur a firm ridge down his back. When he was within reach, she delivered one sharp kick into the animal's body.

His yelp of pain and my cry of outrage came simultaneously, but Doris was unheeding. Her blow had forced the big dog half out the doorway and now she whirled, using both hands to push the door shut. My guardian, my protector, was now unable to help me. I was trapped in my own bedroom with a murderer.

"You're wrong," she repeated, striding over to the dresser. "It wasn't my idea. Jim approached me with the plan. He asked me to pave the way with Henry. He knew Henry would listen to me."

In one swift motion, she pulled out the dresser's middle drawer and flipped it over, scattering my socks all over the floor. Taped to the bottom of the drawer was a file folder. Doris looked up slowly, deliberately.

"You should play poker, Gretchen. You've got the face for it."

Damning praise.

"Why did you keep the papers? Why keep them here?" I was incredulous.

Doris worked the tape off the folder, tossing the empty drawer aside. "What would you have me do? Start a bonfire in my room? I thought the papers were safe. Henry was in prison. Who ever would have guessed John would get all fired up and ruin everything? I came as soon as I heard he was here. But, then." She waved a hand in my direction.

"So was I," I finished her sentence.

"Indeed." She paused and took a moment

to look, amazingly, contrite. "Truly, Gretchen, I didn't know in the beginning that the land was bad. I thought it was a legitimate opportunity."

I scoffed at this, and anger flared in her eyes. She clenched her hands into fists at her sides, crinkling the folder, and beneath her heavy makeup, her face flushed. "Believe me or not, I don't care. I certainly don't owe an explanation to a gold digger like you. But it is the truth!"

We squared off like gunslingers, me over at the big window, she at the foot of the bed. About six feet separated us, but it felt like six inches. The heat of her anger was nearly visible, like waves rising above the highway on a hot summer afternoon.

"By the time it was clear there would be trouble, it was too late. Jim just laughed when I told him he would have to make good on the deal. He didn't care what Henry thought —"

"But you did," I cut in, inching forward ever so slightly. A vague plan was forming at the back of my mind. I didn't take the time to analyze it. I just kept talking. "What did you think, Doris? That Henry would cut you and Bert out of the will!"

"Well, he might have!"

Shifting one foot, I moved another centimeter closer to Doris. "I've only met the man once, Doris, and I know he would never be deliberately cruel or vengeful. Didn't you have any faith in Henry? Or in Bert, for that matter, to protect you?"

At Bert's name, she shrugged. "Bert is useless in an argument. And he has absolutely no head for business."

I didn't bother pointing out that she obviously didn't either.

"If it were up to Bert, our money would be in a savings account! He never wants to take a chance! Be aggressive! Be bold! That's why I've always handled our business affairs. Not that I've wanted to, mind you, but by default."

I would have been a fool not to realize Doris never did anything by default. She'd never do anything she didn't want to do. So, she must have really wanted to murder Jim Gallagher.

"You said Gallagher laughed at you. When was that? That night in the woods? That night you claimed you saw Al's brother?"

"I did see Don. Not that night, though. I saw him the night before, hovering on the edge of the woods like some sort of peeping Tom." Her nose curled in derision, and she paused, her eyes meeting mine in a calculating glance. "You're so smart, Gretchen. Or, at least, you think you are. Tell me your theory. Tell me how I killed Jim Gallagher, and I'll tell you where you're wrong."

So, we were to play a game, it seemed.

"And will you tell me when I'm right?"

Doris tipped her head to one side, considering. Her fingers moved in their rhythmic pattern up and down the length of her eyeglass chain. The repetitive motion was hypnotic. I had to blink and look away.

"Of course, I'll tell you when you're right. That would only be fair." Smiling, she went on with deadly logic, "Because no matter what you know or what I say, it'll be my word against yours. You'll never be able to prove a thing. You have no evidence."

I dropped my eyes to the papers she held, and she flapped them at me.

"Oh, rest assured, I'll burn these as soon as I leave this room." Her eyes flashed. "I'll burn down this whole house if I have to."

I didn't doubt it.

I curled my fingers more tightly around the brass button I still held, feeling its pointed loop poke my skin.

Catching the motion, Doris gave a dry chuckle. "You don't really think you'll get a conviction based on one little button. A button you can't even prove belongs to me."

Pressing my lips together, I made no reply.

To my astonished eyes, Doris eased herself gently onto the edge of my bed, setting the folder down on the pillow and smoothing the coverlet beneath her fingers before waving me on, like the Queen commanding a musician to play.

I cleared my throat and took another step so I now stood in front of the big armoire. Across the room, the mirror reflected this interesting tableau. If one didn't know better, one might have mistaken us for friends, exchanging confidences in the relaxed privacy of the bedroom. But we were not and never would be friends, and the information we had to exchange would remain secret no longer.

"Well, go on!" Doris prodded impatiently.

"You called Gallagher and asked him to meet you in the woods to discuss the financial fiasco."

With a sigh, Doris commented, "I thought we'd already established that. Go on." Another wave of her bejeweled fingers.

I opened my mouth to continue, then stopped, sniffing the air surreptitiously. Was there a hint of violet in the air? Was my poor overwrought brain malfunctioning at a crucial time?

"When he laughed at your concern, you — what? — threatened him?" I guessed.

"Cold," Doris shook her head. "Try again."

"Pleaded. Begged."

A stout laugh was the reply. "Never! Colder still. One more try or the game is over, Gretchen. Fair warning."

What would happen when the game was over? I tried again. "He rebuffed you and you flew at him in a rage."

Doris clapped her hands. "Oh, very good. Well done! You're definitely warmer." Twisting her fingers around the eyeglass chain, she seemed to be speaking to herself when she added, "He walked away from me. He had the audacity to turn on his heel and leave me standing there with my finger in my ear."

No one, it seemed, should ever dare to dismiss Doris Honeycutt.

"So, you hit him with your purse?" I didn't give her time to laugh. "Or with a log. Plenty of those in the woods."

Doris' meticulously coiffed head bobbed up and down. "Plenty." The word hung in the air with the weight of true confessions.

I swallowed, suddenly aware of how dry my throat was. Taking in a deep breath to steady my nerves, I detected once more the faint aroma of violets in the air.

"Oh, Auntie —" I began softly.

"What? Speak up!" Doris barked the command.

Not wanting to share, I said, "And he — went down like a ton of bricks."

Catching my eye and holding me like a cat with a mouse, Doris commented, "He did, indeed."

I was the first to blink and look away. "But Gallagher was strangled, besides being hit on the head. Wasn't the log enough to kill him? Or did you just lose it — lose control and throttle him?"

Doris began a tinkling cascade of laughter, so I hurried on.

"You broke your eyeglass chain then. I'm surprised you didn't notice at the time. Don has it now."

She shuddered in distaste. "That would figure. Of course I noticed! I looked everywhere." Her eyes drifted off as she repeated, "Everywhere."

"I can just see you, you know. Straddling this man who is probably unconscious but who has done you this huge disservice."

"Oh, you can, can you?" She placed one hand at the base of her throat, still laughing. "I never lose control, dear. Everything I do is thought out and logical."

"Killing someone isn't very logical."

She shrugged eloquently. "Means to an

end. And now, this conversation is at an end, I'm afraid. Bert will be waiting for me. I left him with specific instructions to pack our things and prepare for our immediate departure." At my startled glance, she added, "We will be leaving the country for an extended vacation abroad as soon as I can make the arrangements. Certainly by the end of the week."

"You can't run away," I pointed out, stepping toward her.

Doris' fingers moved to her eyeglass chain, slipping briskly over the length of it in her habitual fashion.

"That's your plan, Doris? To flee the country?"

Sighing, she repeated, "We will be leaving the country for an extended vacation abroad."

"Call it what you will," I began, then stopped when the overpowering scent of violets wafted past me.

Lifting her head, Doris sniffed the air, and I tensed. "What is that smell?"

Don't ask me what possessed me, at that moment. What ridiculous impulse filled me. I only knew I could not allow this woman to leave the room. Leaving the room seemed tantamount to leaving the country, and that meant more prison time for John's grandfather. That meant a murderer gone free.

As Doris wriggled her nose, her head tipped back to catch the puzzling odor, I coiled, then launched myself at her. For just a few fleeting seconds, the element of surprise was on my side. Doris, stunned, was motionless within my grasp. Then, as comprehension dawned, she began to struggle. We tumbled off the bed and onto the floor, landing in a tangle of arms and legs. The button I held like a talisman slipped from my hand in the fray, and from the corner of my eye I saw it roll across the rug, over near the bedroom door. I also saw, or thought I did — afterwards, I could never be sure — that the bedroom door was no longer securely closed. There was no time to question this peculiar phenomenon now. Doris was bringing her spectator pump down on my calf in a manner guaranteed to bring tears to my eyes and leave bruises that wouldn't fade for weeks.

"Get off me, you stupid girl!" she hissed, practically in my ear. "Have you lost your mind?"

Something sharp poked me in the rib cage, jabbing painfully into my flesh. A gun! My frantic mind deduced erroneously. A heartbeat later, I identified the object accurately as Doris' ubiquitous eyeglasses, their chain now ensnared with the pin on my top.

"You won't get away, Doris," I panted as we wrestled. "I won't let you."

I had the upper hand, being mostly on top of my foe and forty years younger, to boot. But Doris was both clever and resourceful. In a move she must have witnessed during countless hours of television viewing, she lifted her head swiftly, directly, bringing it into a collision course with my own. The force of the blow snapped my head back, making my eyes cross. I went slack.

Doris took advantage of the moment, scrambling to her feet. I saw her sensible shoes with their chunky heels just inches from my bleary eyes. Stretching out one hand, I grasped her ankle, hanging onto the fleshy bit of leg as she attempted to shake me loose.

My head had cleared by now. Looking up at the older woman, I saw her hand reaching into the pocket of her dress. It emerged clutching a small metal cylinder. Too late, I realized what the cylinder contained.

Leaning over me so her eyes were able to look directly into mine, Doris said, "Really, Gretchen, you're worse than that dog. Let go of me!" She wriggled her foot, but I held fast, even as I struggled into a more upright position.

"Don't say I didn't warn you," she taunted, aiming the cylinder and depressing the button on the top.

As the pepper spray hit me, I pinched my eyes shut, hoping to avoid the worst of its impact. Even so, I felt the irritant attacking and let out a howl worthy of Big Nick. At the same instant, I sensed rather than felt movement in the air around me. Blinded as I was, I could never be a very good witness as to what happened next and, more importantly, how. All I could ever swear to was that, as Doris depressed the button which sent the stinging, burning spray into my face, there came a crash from across the room as the bedroom window blew open. A cold sharp blast of fresh air passed over me with the force of a gale, then my own howls were joined by those of Doris. The gust had blown a substantial amount of her weapon right back into her face.

I heard the metal container hit the rug as she dropped it, shrieking with what must have been both pain and surprise. Covering my eyes, I tried to blink, but could not. The very idea of actually opening my eyes was unthinkable. My lips stung, I could feel them swelling, and my skin tingled sharply, as if I'd been out in a cold wind for a very long time. Dropping my head down, I rocked back and forth, whimpering.

Vaguely, I became aware of the dratted scent of violets in the air once more. Across the room, the wind banged the pane in a staccato rhythm and, just a few feet away, Doris clawed at the bedroom door. It had been ajar earlier in our conversation. Now, I heard it swish gently over the rug as it came fully open. The next sound wasn't as easy to identify. Shuffling. Scuttling. I strained to hear, but the depth of my own pain dimmed my other senses. Only later, after the fact, could I determine the source of the sound. It had been Doris on hands and knees crawling out into the hallway.

As I pulled myself up onto the bed, I could hear thumping in the distance. Thunder? Earth tremor? Some other form of natural disaster?

John told me later what he had seen from the foyer. He said Doris had been standing by the time he saw her. Her eyes were still shut, her cheeks flushed red beneath the heavy layer of her makeup.

"It all happened so quickly," he went on, his voice forlorn, exhausted. "Bert and I were at the foot of the stairs when Al came rushing in, shouting something about you and Doris and waving his arms over his head. We started to go up when we heard the shouting and thumping. Then, all of a sudden, Doris was there, at the top of the stairs, half crying, half shouting. She seemed totally disoriented. It was as if she'd been drugged or something." He broke off to shake his head once more. "It seemed like it happened in slow motion, Gretchen. Before we could even rush up the stairs to her, she was on the edge. Bert shouted to her, 'Dorrie, be careful!' and when she heard his voice, she stepped toward him — into thin air."

That was the scene I came upon fifteen minutes later. Bert, huddled over the limp and twisted form of Doris. Even I could tell from the bend at her neck that she was dead. The oddly angled broken leg hardly seemed to matter.

Slowly, too carefully, I descended the staircase, squinting to see. John held out his arms silently, and I went to him, clinging, sobbing, unable to speak. Big Nick's ears heard the siren first. He was at the front door when the ambulance attendants rushed through.

"I called 911," John explained, "but I know it's too late to help her."

"She was the murderer, John. Just like I told you. She killed Jim Gallagher in a fit of rage that night in the woods. She . . . she . . ." My throat closed over another bout of tears, and I let John lead me to the quiet of the library.

"Stay here, darling, and try to relax. I'll be back as soon as I can." He pressed his lips gently to my feverish brow.

By evening, I'd told my story to the police and to a horrified Mary and Al. They had joined John and me at the kitchen table for soothing cups of tea. Poor Bert slept upstairs, sedated under a doctor's order.

"I wonder what she meant to do," Mary pondered aloud. "I mean, would she have killed you to escape?"

Shaking my head, I said, "I don't think so. I think she honestly believed she and Bert could just disappear. Just pretend it had never happened." I turned to John, "And where were you all the while we were having our cozy chat upstairs?" Sarcasm and a blaze of anger lit my words. "You knew my suspicions. Didn't you start to worry when I was gone so long? When Doris was, too?"

He had the decency to look chagrined. "I didn't notice for a long time, Gretchen. I thought you were out on another of your walks. And then Bert cornered me."

"Bert did? About what?" Mary popped the

question. Beside her, Al poured a great quantity of sugar into his tea, stirring and nodding.

"Apparently Doris had issued orders to pack their things, just as Gretchen told us. He had already been noticing behavior out of the ordinary in his wife and this pushed him into his own conclusions. He told me he thought Doris knew something about the murder she wasn't telling. He stopped then, but I got the feeling his thoughts went further. I think he'd begun to suspect she was guilty, as well."

Al shook his head. "I'm only sorry I didn't get back to those windows sooner. Just a minute or two, and I could have stopped her. When I got up that ladder and saw her with you in the bedroom — well, I knew there'd be trouble. Always knew this whole business would be trouble."

I took a breath. "Is that why you erased my computer file? To try and stop us from stirring up trouble?"

John looked puzzled, but Al just looked sheepish and guilty.

Mary, at her husband's side, prompted, "Did you do that?"

Al nodded. "Yep. You see," he looked to John, who stirred his tea. "I always thought, well, was afraid. Well, guessed, I guess —"

213

Obviously, he was having a hard time putting his idea into words of confession.

"You thought your brother, Don, did it," John stated bluntly, earning a grateful look from Al.

"You just never know," Al said. "He's always been different. You just never know."

"Don!" Mary exclaimed, amazed. "Don wouldn't hurt a single living thing," she chided.

"Whereas, Doris . . ." John left the sentence hanging.

"Poor Bert," I murmured, tears welling in my eyes.

Mary reached across the table and covered my hand with her own. She gave it a squeeze, and we both began to cry.

CHAPTER
TWENTY-FOUR

The wheels of justice grind slowly, especially when they're grinding in reverse. Eventually though, the four of us piled into Mary and Al's van and headed for the prison to, as John liked to put it, "spring Gramps." The snowy countryside sped past the windows, sparkling in the bright morning air. Mary leaned toward the dashboard, pushing the temperature button up.

"Oh, but it's cold today. Some homecoming it'll be for your grandfather."

"Bet he won't even notice," Al remarked, his eyes unwavering on the road.

Shifting over closer to John, I sighed. "I'll bet it's a lot warmer in Florida. I wonder how Bert's doing there?"

Immediately after Doris' funeral, Bert had gone to visit his brother and sister-in-law in Florida. After the whirlwind of media attention he had had to endure as the story became public, the escape to relative obscurity was welcome. His long-range future remained unknown. Guilty of no crime, he was nevertheless, a marked — and marred — man.

John squeezed my shoulder. "He'll be okay. He's a Honeycutt, after all."

As if that guaranteed anything. It hadn't brought happiness, and it hadn't brought justice. Henry Hanover Honeycutt's release from prison had not been brought about by string-pulling. When I recalled the events leading up to this moment, I shuddered. The last few weeks had been intensely emotional, but at least now they would culminate in a joyful reunion.

And so it was.

The aging gentleman I'd met only once emerged from the gloomy prison looking thinner than before but with something very much like a spring in his step. He stood stock still just outside the prison entrance, his eyes drifting upward, sweeping over the landscape, taking in sky, sunshine, a few clouds — and freedom. Slowly, the old man blinked, as if returning from somewhere far away. Then, he focused on the vehicle approaching him. A broad smile cracked his face as he recognized the van. John had flung open the door and hit the ground running before Al had even turned off the engine.

Mary, Al and I hung back, standing beside the van and watching as grandfather and grandson embraced.

Henry clapped John on the back, pulled away to examine his face, then hugged him once more. When John reached up and swiped a hand over his eyes, brushing away tears, my throat swelled, and my eyes brimmed over. Beside me, Al shifted and snorted, clearing his throat noisily. Mary groped for my hand, crunching the fingers painfully as she fought her own tears.

Henry laughed, reached into his pocket and produced a handkerchief. Taking a moment to blow his nose, John then led his grandfather to the van, carrying the satchel that held the older man's few belongings. More hugs, more kisses, more tears followed until at last the cheery ex-con asked, "Can we go home now? I'd like to get away from this place before they change their minds and haul me back in!"

With John gingerly supporting one elbow, Henry climbed into the van, and the rest of us followed suit. As we turned out of the prison gate and onto the highway, Henry demanded of John, "Now, I know you told me everything, but tell me again. Go slowly."

Taking turns, we went over old ground, each adding details as the story unfolded. By the time we reached the sad end of the tale, Henry was shaking his head, in amazement or dismay, I couldn't be sure.

"This button you stepped on, Gretchen, how did it get there — in the middle of the rug?"

I shrugged. "No idea. It was Doris' button, and she usually stayed in my room when visiting. It must have come loose during her struggle with Gallagher, falling off once she got home. But as for how it came to be out in plain sight —" I pursed my lips and shook my head.

"I vacuumed and swept that room just the other day," Mary said, "but I don't remember sweeping any buttons from under the bed." She frowned. "And I've cleaned your room plenty of times since the murder anyway."

"And that gale wind," Henry leaned toward me. "Coming from nowhere. What about that?"

Having already related those details, I opened my mouth, then shut it again.

"The latch on the window was cracked," Al told us. "It was old, weakened by age. Force of that wind just snapped it. Plain and simple."

I exchanged a glance with Mary, then John, then Henry.

"Did you . . ." Henry began, then paused. "Now Gretchen, humor an old man. Did you smell anything when it happened? Something, well, flowery?"

There it was, the detail I'd deliberately left out. No one would believe that Auntie's ghost came to my aid, providing a clue, then saving my life and helping to end Doris'.

Nodding once, twice, then faster and faster, I said, "Yes! Both times I smelled the violets. Both times!"

Sitting back, looking drained but pleased, Henry said, "Thought so."

"It isn't logical to think a ghost, a presence of some otherworldly source, brought these events about," John told us, sounding academic. "And yet, that's what you believe, isn't it?"

"Have you got a better explanation?" Mary asked as her husband scoffed.

Slapping his hand against the steering wheel, Al repeated, "The window lock was old and weak. The end."

"Hmm," Henry hummed, then changed the subject. "And the book, John, how's it going?"

"Slowly, but we'll pick up speed now, I think."

"Slowly." He nodded. "Good. That means you'll be with us for the foreseeable future, then, Gretchen?"

I looked to John for my answer. "I think so. That is, uh —"

"She will," John interrupted, as the van seemed to fill with a very expectant silence. "And well beyond that, I'm hoping." He looked into my eyes questioningly, and I took a deep breath that caught in my throat.

Coughing, I said, "Umm, yes. I have a clear calendar. No other job offers —"

Mary's hoot of sudden laughter cut me off. "Gretchen, you ninny, he's not talking about the job!"

In true bewilderment, I turned anxious eyes to John. A dawning realization grew into a knot in my stomach and a flutter in my heart. "Well, what then?" I asked, knitting my brows.

John took me in his arms as best he could in the confines of the van. Just before he kissed me, he said, "Here, I'll give you a clue."

Over the singing in my ears, I heard Henry Hanover Honeycutt say, "Now, there's a happy ending!"

ABOUT THE AUTHOR

Kate Fellowes has always lived in the Upper Midwest, earning her degree from Alverno College in Milwaukee. Her working life has revolved around words — editor of the student newspaper, reporter for the local press, cataloger in her hometown library. She is the author of three previous novels of romantic suspense and numerous short stories and essays. Married, she and her husband share their home with a variety of companion animals. They live near the shore of Lake Michigan.

We hope you have enjoyed this Large Print book. Other Thorndike, Wheeler, and Chivers Press Large Print books are available at your library or directly from the publishers.

For information about current and upcoming titles, please call or write, without obligation, to:

Publisher
Thorndike Press
295 Kennedy Memorial Drive
Waterville, ME 04901
Tel. (800) 223-1244

or visit our Web site at:

http://gale.cengage.com/thorndike

OR

Chivers Large Print
published by BBC Audiobooks Ltd
St James House, The Square
Lower Bristol Road
Bath BA2 3SB
England
Tel. +44(0) 800 136919
email: bbcaudiobooks@bbc.co.uk
www.bbcaudiobooks.co.uk

All our Large Print titles are designed for easy reading, and all our books are made to last.